LEAD FROM THE FRONT

Inspiring military stories of courage, leadership and resilience

SUDEEP KRISHNA
PURAV GANDHI

INDIA • SINGAPORE • MALAYSIA

Copyright © Sudeep Krishna, Purav Gandhi 2024
All Rights Reserved.

ISBN 979-8-89233-773-1

This book has been published with all efforts taken to make the material error-free after the consent of the author. However, the author and the publisher do not assume and hereby disclaim any liability to any party for any loss, damage, or disruption caused by errors or omissions, whether such errors or omissions result from negligence, accident, or any other cause.

While every effort has been made to avoid any mistake or omission, this publication is being sold on the condition and understanding that neither the author nor the publishers or printers would be liable in any manner to any person by reason of any mistake or omission in this publication or for any action taken or omitted to be taken or advice rendered or accepted on the basis of this work. For any defect in printing or binding the publishers will be liable only to replace the defective copy by another copy of this work then available.

Dedicated to the memory of some of
India's greatest leaders who helped shape
this country into what it has become today

Contents

Acknowledgements 7

Introduction 9

1. A Well-Oiled Machine 13
2. Forged in Fire 33
3. The Bal is in Our 'Kot' 47
4. Unlimited Liability 61
5. Fortune Favours the Brave 73
6. INS Resilience 87
7. Thappad se Dar Nahi Lagta 103
8. Turning the Tide 121
9. The Men Who Saw Tomorrow 139

About the Authors 157

Acknowledgements

We owe a deep debt of gratitude to all the leaders featured in this book. They openly welcomed us into their homes and their hearts. The most common phrase that they uttered when we asked them to share their stories, was - 'Who would be interested in my story?'. They took time from their busy schedules and participated in multiple review cycles. Recognizing that two civilians were trying to write military stories, they patiently corrected facts and spent time explaining the technical aspects of their day-to-day work. If there are any errors in the way the stories are represented, those errors are ours alone.

We specifically would like to call out the help and support provided by Col S Vijay Kumar, SM. Vijay is a dear friend and is known to the authors for a long time. He made the initial set of connections for us and helped us a lot with access to the NDA, while he was serving there.

As we finalized the stories, we felt the need to run these by some potential readers to get their input. A huge thank you to Ishita Gupta, Isha Talsania, Grishma Thaker, Urmil Shah, Prachi Chimmwal, Sachin Baghadiya, Aditya Dave, Vatsala Sudeep, and many others for their help reviewing and shaping these stories.

Acknowledgements

Last but not the least, this book would not have seen the light of the day without support from our families. The authors were both in full time jobs while this book was taking shape. The travel to different parts of the country, hunting for stories and the related meetings, happened on the weekends. This time spent away from families meant that someone else had to step in and pick up the slack. Maitri, Haritha, our kids and parents - this book belongs as much to you as it belongs to us.

– Sudeep & Purav

Introduction

With a collective 35+ years of experience in the corporate world, we have seen our share of good and bad leaders. As we grew in our respective careers and into leadership roles, we asked ourselves a simple question: "What makes a leader great?" The search for an answer led us on a journey across a vast leadership universe that culminated in the fascinating world of the Indian Armed Forces. We heard many riveting stories about life in the armed forces, how leaders are made, and how they are tested in demanding conditions. From these conversations came the idea of writing a book to bring these stories to life.

This book is the culmination of a five-year effort. We visited multiple cantonments, Air Force stations, and training institutes hunting for stories and the lessons they represent. We also got the opportunity to spend time at the LoC (Line of Control, the border between India and Pakistan) in Kashmir, trying to understand the conditions in which our soldiers live and fight. We thought this was important for us to do because 4 of the 9 stories in this book reference the LoC or Kashmir.

Contrary to popular belief, leaders in the armed forces are not always fighting wars. They will spend 90% of their career in a combination of field and peace postings, honing their skills and learning how to lead those missions when they 'might' face the enemy. However, these periods are heavily interspersed with mundane administrative tasks, field exercises, fitness drills, and people management. As a part of that career journey, they have aspirations similar to the ones that we have. Sustained career growth, better perks and compensation, a comfortable life for their families, and good career prospects for their children.

We have detailed some 'war stories' like 'A well-oiled machine'- exploits of a Company Commander and his team in the dark jungles of Kupwara and 'The Bal is in our Kot'- drawing a deep insight into the mind of a fighter pilot who led a part of the Balakot bombing mission. We also covered some 'non-war' stories like 'Turning the Tide', where a young Captain transforms his company of soldiers from mediocre troops to outstanding warriors.

We also talk about the vision of a former Vice Chief of the Indian Airforce and one of his commanding officers who together reactivated the disused Daulat Beg Oldie (DBO) airstrip, without waiting for any official approvals. That one bold move in 2008 continues to act as a force multiplier and saved countless lives during the ongoing face-off against China that started in 2020. And just to acknowledge that even some of the best leaders make mistakes, we write a humorous take on how a militant got the better of an over-enthusiastic officer in 'Thappad se dar nahin lagta'.

We wrote this book as stories because each of our readers might draw different lessons from them. Some of you might read these stories for inspiration, whereas some might read them for entertainment. Either way, we hope you enjoy reading this book as much as we have enjoyed bringing these stories to life.

Chapter 1
A Well-Oiled Machine

A high-performing, well-trained team, led by a strong leader, works seamlessly to achieve its objectives. And in many cases, the leaders of such teams have a strong **bias for action**. They consider available information, trust their instincts, and are decisive. They then act and drive their teams to execute previously rehearsed plans with pinpoint accuracy and discipline. Captain Kapil's story, set in the unforgiving jungles in the higher reaches of the Kupwara district in Kashmir, illustrates a similar bias for action and disciplined execution.

It was a cold and dark night when Captain Kapil Sinha first arrived at Kupwara. He was excited at getting his first posting so close to the border. It meant some action for sure. But after four uneventful months, Captain Sinha felt disappointed. After all, he had heard stories about the upper reaches of Kupwara from his seniors at the IMA and was looking forward to his posting. "All the bloody Kachra gets flushed there," Major Rawat once told him over a bottle of scotch and cigarettes. The Major was also a Captain when he was posted in the valley. "If Kashmir is Jannat, then the upper reaches of Kupwara is Jahannum."

But for Captain Sinha, just like everyone in the Army, duty preceded everything in life, and he was trained to follow orders. Jahannum or not, if he was told to lead his men there, that is what he would exactly do.

Situated in the northwest region of Kashmir, Kupwara was one of the closest regions to the Line of Control. From some of the villages in Kupwara, you could see the other side of the border, Pakistan-occupied Kashmir (POK). The roads were higher, and the vehicles crawled like ants moving across an anthill. Pine and Deodar trees populated the region and stood like tall, eerie shadows on both sides of the valley once it became dark. Visibility was zero on most nights, especially when it snowed. And it snowed relentlessly during winters.

But these parts were heavily guarded and were relatively safer. As one moved towards Northern Kupwara, towards the higher ground, things became murkier. The trees became scarier, and the whole landscape looked sinister. "It's cold and dark, and you don't want to be surrounded by the woods," one of his seniors had told him. This was perhaps why terrorists preferred this route to infiltrate into the valley. Plus, the mountainous terrain was infamous for avalanches, making it impossible for the Indian Army to put up a fence. It was the perfect entry point for terrorists.

Major Rawat once narrated the story about how he earned his spurs in the regiment. "When I was posted there, we got reports of militants in the area. As we moved through the woods, we lost all visibility. I could not see my hands in front of me, so I fell on my knees and started crawling. After a few minutes, I felt something clash against my AK. Turns out it was another AK, but clearly not one of ours because I was leading, and my men were behind me. I impulsively fired. There was a flash of light in the dark and something whizzed past me. A shadow collapsed on the snow with a loud grunt. It wasn't until morning I realised what had transpired. We had accidentally bumped into the militants. And the one whose AK clashed with mine had also fired but his gun got deflected while mine hit the target."

The Major chuckled. It was a great war story, one that was always narrated with a lot of pride and gusto. Captain Sinha got goosebumps when he first heard it and wondered if he would also have stories that would be told with similar pride and gusto in Army circles.

Captain Sinha's company had 120-odd soldiers. They oversaw about a 5-10 square Km area along the Line of Control (LoC) that had many nullahs. These are dried streams or narrow passes hugging the steep narrow valley and could be used as a hidden passage. However, they became extremely dangerous during winters and rains. The binoculars and guns were pointed towards the enemy's direction 24/7 and even the slightest activity would trigger an alarm in the Indian camp. The tents they used opened at the top where they could stand up and quickly scan the neighbouring areas, including the border and the nearby posts as well.

But the terrorists and militants had become aware of these tactics and hence chose other, less populated nullahs and passes that hugged both India and POK (Pakistan-Occupied Kashmir). They never attacked frequently, especially in an open area like Kupwara where they knew security was tight. Instead, they waited till the soldiers became complacent in their duties, which sometimes happened due to long periods of inactivity and boredom. It was a game of patience that went on for months.

Captain Sinha sighed. It was 8 O'Clock on his wristwatch and he had just finished dinner. After four months of absolute silence, a slight tediousness had silently crept inside the camp. He knew his men were alert, but just like him, they were hungry for action. Except for the occasional visits from stray animals like a leopard or a bear, nothing ever showed up on the motion and heat detectors. He sat and wondered about the bottle of Black Label that was lying at the bottom of his trunk. It had been a parting gift from a fellow officer, and he was waiting for the right moment to crack it open.

He and his men had trained relentlessly over the past three months. They identified possible infiltration routes and placed motion detectors and forward posts across nullahs and routes respectively. He taught his men how to use and test the thermal cameras on multiple occasions. They also practiced ambushes in case any terrorists were detected. One key aspect of their training was fire discipline. A sacred rule in his Battalion, and in the Army in general, was not to fire unless specifically instructed. The officer who trained him at the NDA had a famous quote, "Ek goli-Ek dushman," which meant one bullet for one enemy.

As he thought about his own preparedness and all the hours that his company had put into training, he realised that one or two pegs of his favourite Black Label would not dull his senses. He was confident he could take out a couple of terrorists in combat even after downing half a bottle.

Captain Sinha unlatched the big green steel trunk and retrieved the black bottle. He stared at it for a moment and muttered under his breath, "Beautiful!"

But as he was about to unscrew it, the JCO (Junior Commissioned Officer) walked into his tent with the day's report.

"Saab, except for some bears, there has been no new movement," reported JCO Gaud.

Prashant Gaud was a dark, slim man with a pencil-thin moustache and a seriousness lingering about him. It had been more than 15 years since he joined the regiment as a young sepoy. Today, he was a Naib Subedar, the senior most soldier in his company whom the men looked up to for mentorship and support. Although he was 10 years older than his Captain, in age and experience,

Gaud knew that this young officer had the ability to lead decisively. This relationship between JCOs and the officers is the cornerstone of success in the Indian Army. Each recognises the others' ability to do their duty with honesty and hence uses Saab as a mark of respect. They had an easy-going relationship and often shared jokes when they were together in his tent.

"Bhaloos! That's all the Pakistanis have been sending us."

"Sometimes some Tenduas – Leopards – too, for a change," the JCO said sarcastically.

They both laughed.

"Saab, aaj peg laga hi lo. Have one peg today," said Prashant, eyeing the bottle.

Captain Sinha smiled. "You are right, Saab. Anyways, nothing is happening. Come, you also have one with me."

Prashant accepted the offer and gave a slight nod. There were few moments when he could be at the same level as his Company Commander. In the armed forces, it was all about respecting ranks. The opportunity to sit with his Captain and share a drink did not come every day, especially in a sensitive area like Kupwara.

Captain Sinha pulled out two tin tumblers from his trunk. After unscrewing the cap in one swift motion, he poured out one large peg for his JCO and one small peg for himself.

As he kept the bottle down, the JCO's radio crackled. "....Saab, the motion detector picked up something..."

Prashant clicked his radio. "...Ok..coming.." He put down his tumbler. "Saab, I'll just check and come."

Captain Sinha picked up his tumbler and leaned back on his bed. Bloody Bhaloos.

The distance between one camp and the other was about 500 metres. The Indian soldiers usually avoided the road for fear of ambush. Instead, they walked through the woody forest or wetlands to avoid detection. During winters, a thick fog engulfed the region, and it was impossible to travel unless you knew every corner. JCO Gaud knew every inch, and that is why he could travel quickly without a torch. After a few seconds, he realised that he was not alone. His buddy, a young lanky sepoy, fell in step behind him, bringing the rear of this two-man patrol.

In the Army, there is always someone with you - a buddy - whose job is to follow you around like a shadow. If, in case, the one in charge gets incapacitated or KIA (Killed in Action), then the buddy takes over. The buddy has your back covered. Even when the guards are patrolling during peacetime or moving in their jeeps from one location to another, they will always have someone with them. It is rare for any Army personnel - no matter the rank - to move around on their own.

The only sound came from their thick boots crunching the foliage. After 10 minutes of walking, two tiny lights peeked through the dark trees. Prashant quickened his pace and headed towards them.

There were three tents in a semicircle. Prashant entered the first one. Inside, there were three jawans sitting in front of the equipment.

"Hanji – yes – what can we see?" The JCO asked his men.

"Saab, have a look," said one of the jawans.

Prashant looked at the blinking red lights on the screen. "Accha. Show me the thermal cameras."

"Saab, here," said the jawan who was sitting near another monitor. Prashant saw the green and orange blob on the screen. It was too big for a human. It must be a bear, he thought.

"Hmm," said Prashant and called the Captain. "Saab, it's a Bhaloo."

"I see," the Captain's voice crackled. "And Saab, what about the other posts?"

Prashant sighed a little. If there had been something, they would have reported it already, he thought. "Other posts? I'll check." He radioed two other posts close to them. "Has the motion detector been triggered?" He asked the jawan at post 3.

"Yes," crackled the voice.

"What about the thermal?"

"It's a white blob," the jawan said. "Most probably a bear."

Prashant radioed the other posts and got a similar response from some of them.

He called the Captain.

Captain Sinha stared at the drink and was wondering what Prashant was doing. It was getting chillier by the second, and all he wanted to do was gulp down two drinks and retire for the night. For a change, the whisky would give him some respite from the merciless cold.

Prashant's voice crackled on his radio. "Saab, same thing in both posts. Must be Bhaloos."

Somebody is getting married or what! Kapil thought. "Bhaloo ki poori baraat nikli hain aaj raat." "The bears have let out a marriage procession."

The moment Captain Sinha uttered these words, he realised the stupidity of it. Do Bhaloos hunt at night? Maybe. But what are the chances of sighting three different Bhaloos in three separate posts at the same time?

And then, like lightning, it hit him. The Pakistanis have not sent Bhaloos this time.

He quickly radioed Prashant. "Saab, alert all the posts. We will be busy tonight for a change."

Captain Sinha slipped the Beretta into the holster. He picked up his AK and walked out of the tent. The two tumblers of Black Label whisky lay untouched on his table.

The night grew colder. A thick fog had now condensed around the pines, cedars, and spruces. At times, the bark of a fox or the low growls of a leopard pierced the still night. Wild dogs and leopards often attacked people in that region, but Captain Sinha was least bothered. Before leaving, he had radioed all the posts to do a thorough scanning of the place - motion detectors, thermal cameras, night vision cameras, and every other equipment that they had.

He and his buddy started sprinting towards the post where Prashant was monitoring the situation. Upon reaching, he was told that similar blobs had sprung up at many posts and that they were all converging near one of the empty passes by the side of the hill. This was a blind spot. However, once they crossed the hill, they would have to expose themselves in the open area.

Captain Sinha knew that. Even the terrorists did. But they also knew that they were expendable, unlike the Indian soldiers who had to do everything in their power to stay alive and eliminate the enemy.

As he scanned the images, he saw that the different blobs converged in one area and started moving toward the pass in a single file. There were 9 terrorists, he surmised. They would probably cross the hill in 60 minutes or so before arriving at the open area. It could be the perfect ambush point for my men.

"Ok, so everyone knows what we need to do?" The Captain asked coolly.

"Ji Saab. Yes Sir," Everyone replied.

"Saab, we don't have much time," the Captain said, turning to Prashant. He laid down a map on the table and pointed to a region. "We have trained for this moment for the past three months. Let's quickly set up an ambush in this open area and ensure that all angles of fire are covered."

"Ji Saab," Prashant said and immediately started passing instructions to the other posts.

A Well-Oiled Machine

After his JCO left, Captain Sinha wondered how this night would turn out. Encounters in Kupwara were always a battle of attrition. The terrorists kept coming in numbers to wear down the limited number of soldiers posted at the border. Some operations lasted more than a week as the terrorists used the thick jungles to escape. Casualties were recorded on both sides, but the Indian Army was hurt more every time one of their men fell in battle.

Prashant returned within a few minutes. "Saab, the men are ready. The primary team will lay and execute the ambush. The backup team will outflank these terrorists and cut their escape path so they don't run back into POK".

"Good," the Captain said and walked out towards the group that Prashant had gathered. He looked at the young faces in front of him. These were the jawans who unquestioningly stood in the cold for months and silently followed orders. Some of them might not come back alive tonight.

"Sab taiyaar? Everyone ready?" The Captain said.

"Taiyaar Saab!" Came the swift reply in unison. "Ready Sir!"

"The Pakistanis want to play tonight. Let's welcome the guests."

The men started walking north, towards the rendezvous. The Captain had a muted smile. He may only be 24 years old, but everyone in the Army knew there was no age restriction to either kill or be killed. This is going to be my story, the Captain promised himself.

The night vision goggles made it easier to navigate in the dark, but they still walked slowly. At the end of the woody area, the Captain silently ordered his men to spread out. Beyond this was the clearing. Like Ninjas, the men stealthily moved and strategically positioned themselves, hiding behind trees and bushes. The Captain and Prashant also positioned themselves behind two trees.

At this time of the hour, visibility was practically zero. Captain Sinha knew that they would have to rely on night vision, their ears, and intuition. From where they were standing, it could mean death if they strayed from the plan for even a fraction of a second. The infiltrators would fire blindly, and the chances of catching a stray bullet were high.

It was some time before they heard a noise. It could have been mistaken for a rabbit or fox, but the Captain could hear faint voices. Even though they were muted, they were definitely human voices. One of them was shushing the others. He waited and stared at his watch. It would take 5 minutes for someone to cross the firing zone. As their night vision improved, they could now see the silhouettes. Nine weary, dangerous men slowly made their way across the open ground.

For a moment Captain Sinha fought back a mild bout of panic. This was the moment when a young jawan with a nervous trigger finger could fire early, thereby dispersing the terrorists and inviting retaliation. But the training held. All his men patiently waited for his signal.

When exactly 3 minutes had passed, on their Captain's signal, the Indian troops opened fire. The roar of multiple AK's took the unsuspecting terrorists by surprise. Some of them did not even get the time to point their guns in the right direction. A few of them had dropped to the ground, but Sinha's men calmly ensured that their fire was concentrated and deadly. It was a great display of firing discipline, something the terrorists lacked. Not a single bullet was fired at Captain Sinha's men. To some, it might have felt like an eternity, but the whole thing was over in a matter of minutes.

In his night vision, Captain Sinha saw 8 bodies lying motionless on the cold ground. The ninth one was squirming. His team walked towards the last terrorist. Someone flashed a light. He removed his night vision goggles and stared at the young face. It was a boy, no more than 15 or 16. Captain Sinha was confident that he was most likely a guide who was helping these terrorists cross. There was no gun or any other weapon on him. There was a high chance that he was a Kashmiri whose family had been threatened or even kidnapped for safe passage into Indian soil.

"Aur kitne hai?" Asked the Captain. "How many more are there?"

The boy wriggled in pain and muttered, "Bas, bas, aur koi nahin hai. That's it, there are no more."

The sensors and the backup team confirmed that the boy was speaking the truth. The terrorists usually came in small batches and they moved as a tight group. So, it was likely that apart from this batch no other members were lurking around. And even if they had somehow magically evaded the Indian Army's surveillance, their fate would be no different from the ones lying on the ground. Captain Sinha and all the officers who would come after him would make sure of that.

"Saab, what do we do with him?" asked Prashant. "Shall we…"

"No need," replied the Captain calmly. "We will take him for pooch taach – interrogation."

The JCO ordered the jawans to carry the boy for medical treatment.

After everyone left, Captain Sinha stayed back and surveyed the ambush area. The sound of gunshots reverberated in his ear. Such operations took along such thin margins that anyone in his place would have felt lucky to stay alive. But not him, though. He did not congratulate himself or his men on their achievements. For him, it was a routine job that anyone in his place would have done.

That night, multiple radio sets crackled across the Indian side of the LoC, swiftly carrying the news of a successful operation.

At dawn, a group of senior Army leaders descended on the area. Leading that contingent was the Northern Army commander, the senior most General in charge of all the operations in North India. He was a heavily built man in his late fifties whose purposeful gait was immediately recognised by everyone from a distance.

Upon arriving at the scene, he was amazed at how seamlessly the operation was planned and how quickly it had been executed. Having served in the valley for ages, the General knew that ambushes go south in the blink of an eye. But the fact that not a single drop of Indian blood had been spilt left him in awe of Captain Sinha's leadership.

The General appreciated the men and pulled Captain Sinha aside. "Son, in my nearly 40 long years of service, I have not seen an operation where the enemy did not even get a chance to fire back at us. You and your men have made us all proud today."

A sudden surge of gratitude for his men spread through Captain Sinha's veins. Braving extreme odds, his men had delivered an outstanding result. Staying true to their training, they operated as one well-oiled machine. Every little piece in their machinery, including the jawans, performed exactly as they were supposed to and ensured that this juggernaut pierced through the hearts of terrorists.

The General continued, "I will honour your Battalion with a unit citation, and I will also recommend you for a Shaurya Chakra."

Shaurya Chakra! Captain Sinha was stunned. The Shaurya Chakra is India's third-highest peacetime gallantry award. It is given only to the bravest Army personnel and elevates the recipient in the eyes of his peers and soldiers. His mind immediately went back to other SC winners like Late Lt. Col. Udhe Singh, Sep. PO Ommen, and Maj. Kamal Kalia, whose stories enthralled him during his NDA days. Captain Sinha thought that his story would also be told to young recruits in the regiment.

A wide smile spread across his face, and he held his head a little higher.

The Lt. Gen. broke the silence. "And while all these recommendations make their way through the Army bureaucracy, here is a little something for you as a token of my appreciation for the way you led."

Captain Sinha was mildly surprised as he received a nicely wrapped package from his General. But it soon turned into a wide grin, and he even let out a laugh. "Sir, this feels like a full circle."

Inside the neatly wrapped package was a bottle of Johnny Walker Black Label.

Author's Note: Captain, now Colonel Kapil Sinha, (name changed on request) continues to serve in the Indian Army. He has become a legend in his regiment and an inspiration for new officers and other recruits. His consistent leadership track record has positioned him for strong leadership roles in the Army, including a stint at the prestigious National Defence Academy, where he passed out many years ago as a young Cadet. The NDA is where the authors met him for the first time. The details around this meeting and Col Sinha's insights on how the Indian Armed Forces grow leaders are covered in the next chapter.

Chapter 2
Forged in Fire

Are leaders born? Or are they made? This question is a subject of many debates in our world. However, in the armed forces, **leaders are made**, initially in the officer training institutes and eventually through real-life on-the-job experiences. As young officers, when they lead soldiers into battle, good leadership is often the difference between life and death. In this story, we will get a glimpse of life at the National Defence Academy, India's premier cradle of military leadership, where young men and women, over a 3-year period, grow from wide-eyed students to future military leaders.

There are certain moments in our lives when we feel so inclined towards a goal that we chase it till it becomes ours. We felt a similar inclination, or rather a strong pull, towards Kapil's story when we heard of it for the first time. It became our mission to visit the place where his journey began i.e., The National Defence Academy (NDA), and hear more details about the operation straight from the horse's mouth.

The NDA is, after all, where almost all the finest officers in our country start their journey. Established in 1954 and located in Khadakwasla, Pune, Maharashtra, it is one of the most prestigious military training institutions in the country and also the first stop for cadets of the Indian Army, Navy, and Air Force before they are sent to their respective service academies for further pre-commissioning training.

The selection process for the NDA is highly competitive and is based on a written examination, followed by an interview and a medical examination. The written examination is conducted twice a year by the Union Public Service Commission (UPSC) and is open to candidates who have completed their 10+2 education.

The academy is spread over an area of about 7,015 acres and comprises various training facilities such as a parade ground, sports fields, swimming pools, and firing ranges. When we drove through the front gates for the very first time, we were reeled into the grandiosity almost immediately. Majestic replicas of India's best war machines - fighter planes, tanks, and warships - that help guard our borders greeted us in all their grandeur. As we crossed them and moved ahead, the small NDA airport slowly came into view, where budding officers of the Indian Air Force learn how to fly as cadets. Further down the road, we came across various training centres and eventually the Cadet's mess where over 1,800 cadets are fed 3 meals a day. The dinner service, although we did not witness it, is apparently a sight to behold as all 1,800 cadets are fed almost simultaneously, and is considered to be Asia's largest sit-and-dine. The whole process lasts only a few minutes and is a testament to the military discipline that is drilled into the young cadets from their first day.

Right after the Cadet's mess, the regal Sudan Block headlines the cluster of administrative buildings and classrooms. During World War II, the Indian troops fought on behalf of the British Army to liberate Sudan from the Axis powers. To thank the Indian troops, Sudan gave a gift of 1,00,000 British pounds, of which 70,000 went to India and 30,000 to Pakistan. The Indian Army was in the process of establishing the NDA at that time and, hence, decided to dedicate an important building to all the soldiers who lost their lives for the liberation of Sudan.

On either side of the central road from the Sudan Block, there are smaller roads that lead to squadrons. Squadrons are basically hostels that a Cadet will occupy for the duration of his or her stay at the NDA. There are currently 18 squadrons, and each of them has close to 120 cadets. Even though the NDA was traditionally a male-only institution, in 2022, it welcomed its first batch of female cadets. It's an initiative that was long overdue.

The cadets at the NDA undergo a rigorous training programme that prepares them mentally and physically for the challenges of being an officer in the Indian Armed Forces. The NDA provides a common syllabus for the cadets of all 3 services and includes academic, physical, and military training. The academic training covers subjects such as mathematics, physics, chemistry, English, and general knowledge, while the physical training includes activities such as running, swimming, gymnastics, and obstacle courses. The military training includes drills, weapons training, and map reading.

The NDA also places a strong emphasis on character building and inculcates values such as integrity, loyalty, and duty. The academy provides opportunities for the cadets to participate in extracurricular activities such as sports, music, and drama.

The NDA has a strong alumni network, and its graduates have gone on to hold key positions in the Indian Armed Forces and other government organisations. Some of the notable alumni of the NDA include former Chief of Army Staff General J.J. Singh, former Chief of Naval Staff Admiral R.H. Tahiliani, and former Chief of Air Staff Air Chief Marshal A.Y. Tipnis.

Calling the NDA majestic would be an understatement. We felt a great sense of pride to be there because we knew what it took to be accepted at the NDA. It was not merely cracking an exam and getting into college. The NDA gave a three-year bachelor's degree but more importantly, it taught people to be impactful leaders.

We arrived exactly at 10 am on Sunday as instructed. It was the only day outsiders were allowed to visit after taking prior permission from the Colonel Administration.

We knew punctuality was sacred on NDA grounds and wanted to honour it. We were ushered into the officer's mess. As we sat down, a young man, no older than us, glided towards us in swift motions. He was lean of medium height and moved as straight as an arrow. Kapil exuded a quiet, almost casual confidence, and one could never guess that he was the head of a critical department at the NDA or the fact that he had been honoured with a Shaurya Chakra.

Kapil exchanged pleasantries with us. We eased into the discussion talking about his amazing heroics at Kupwara and how it inspired us to write about the Indian Armed Forces. He was almost embarrassed. "I was just doing my job guys. Anyone else in my place would have done the same."

Despite his humility, we knew that it wasn't a spur-of-the-moment decision. What he displayed in the months leading up to that decisive moment in the jungles of Kupwara was exemplary leadership, something that is drilled into the cadets and future officers at the NDA. And we were keen to learn more about his journey and what made him a good leader.

"It all started here," he said, reminiscing about his early days as a Cadet at the NDA almost 15 years ago. "Every kid in India who dreams of joining the Army, Navy, or Air Force wants to come to the NDA. But only about 350 get selected out of lakhs who apply."

The competition to get into the NDA can be compared to institutions like AIIMS, IITs, or the IIMs. After completing the 3-year course comprising 6 terms, the Cadet will graduate from the NDA with a BSc or BA degree for which they have taken classes and completed the curriculum. And then they will spend a year at a specialised institution relevant to their arm. For example, the Army cadets go to the Indian Military Academy (IMA), the Navy cadets to the Indian Naval Academy (INA), and the Air Force cadets go to the Air Force Academy (AFA). After completing a year at these institutions, they graduate and get commissioned as officers.

"I can talk specifically about my journey," Kapil said. "When I joined the NDA and eventually graduated from the IMA, I was trained to lead from day one. In the civilian or corporate world, people evolve to become good leaders over time. It's almost trial and error. In our case, we cannot take such chances because the lives of the soldiers you command are at stake. Hence, it is way more rigorous than what you folks would have experienced in college."

"And in any case, they don't teach you live firing in college, do they?" Kapil asked with a mischievous smile, looking at our surprised expressions.

Kapil explained, "During training, especially at the IMA, they fire live rounds to condition you. They will dig a ditch that you need to cross, and 6 inches above you, they will fire live bullets. If you get up, you are dead. You must overcome the urge to put your head up even if you are uncomfortable with crawling. You are also trained to ignore the whizzing of the bullets passing by."

This sort of mental conditioning is critical for a soldier. In live operations, they will be in situations where bullets will whistle past them. The first time it happens, it's human nature to freeze. But in an operation, one cannot afford to do that—the live-fire training conditions soldiers to handle such situations.

Kapil continued, "Outside of academics, there are certain key skills, behaviours, and mindsets that we are looking to develop in our cadets:

"We are taught to manage with little sleep. In some cases, we will face Ragara, or our term for punishment by staying up late till 3 or 4 AM in the morning. The reason behind this is that during deployment you won't get any sleep and so you must learn how to manage with little or no sleep."

"It might seem over the top, but it is an important part of being an officer," Kapil said.

"That is how discipline is enforced on us. In the armed forces, it's all about following the chain of command and you cannot break it no matter what. This is where the hierarchy inside the NDA is important to understand. The first termers are the junior most and the 6th termers are the senior most. So, if your senior tells you to do something, you must do it without complaining. The ones above you are there to teach you how to respect authority. Our room and clothes were checked. We were taught how to sit, how to eat, how to use a knife and fork, and every little thing that makes a true officer and a lady/gentleman. As a Cadet, we could not walk inside the NDA. We either marched, jogged, or cycled. If we have a cycle, then we cannot walk it. Either we ride it, run with it, or carry it."

Kapil smiled as an old memory of him as a Cadet flashed by. "Let me tell you a funny incident that happened to me as a first termer. I got delayed at the library and was rushing back to the squadron. It was nearly sundown, and I was worried that I would get punished because I was late. As I reached the squadron courtyard, in the dim light, I saw people rolling on the ground and doing push-ups, typical ragada punishment activity.

As it is the destiny of a first termer to get punished continuously, I quickly put my books aside and joined the group. After 30 minutes of solid ragada, we were asked to stand at attention, and the seniors did a roll call. They found that there was an extra Cadet in the group. As I looked at the faces around me, I was alarmed to notice that the cadets being punished were all fourth-termers. When I joined the NDA, I told myself that I would stay under the radar and out of trouble in my first term. As you can imagine, I was selected for special treatment that whole term by the amused sixth termers and angry fourth-termers who were made fun of by their seniors."

We couldn't stop laughing, with Kapil laughing the loudest.

"Oh, and food was always a problem for us. It's not like they underfed us. The expected calorie intake for a Cadet is nearly 5,000 calories per day, and the food was amazing, but we were always hungry."

"As junior termers, after the morning fall-in, ragada, and random individual punishments, by the time we were able to get to the Cadet's mess, there was very little time to eat. Sometimes, we would steal bread or rotis during meals which we could have later. But even then, we did not get our fill."

Kapil explained that this too was a part of the conditioning that a Cadet goes through.

"Absence of food, constant discomfort, and unexpected punishments prepared cadets for life as an officer in difficult inhospitable conditions, especially during field postings."

We urged Kapil to tell us more about the physical training and conditioning that a Cadet goes through.

"We did all kinds of physical activity. Running for us is what walking is to you. There were obstacle courses, swinging, climbing, jumping, sometimes with load, sometimes without it. We played a lot. Horse riding is compulsory. You know, most games are optional, except horse riding. The horse cavalry maintained by the Indian Army is the world's oldest cavalry. All the other cavalries have now been replaced with tanks. This is one of the ways they inject confidence in cadets. The horses are chalu. They mess with cadets when they feel the Cadet is not confident."

"I also want to spend some time talking about Ustads, the Army havildars who train us," Kapil said, with fondness and respect in his eyes.

"They are the best-enlisted soldiers who are tasked with training the next generation of soldiers and leaders. Some of them have become such legends that they now have dedicated Facebook pages. Generations of military officers including some senior Generals who were trained by these Ustads fondly reminisce about their experiences."

We asked Kapil if he had a favourite ustad story from his time at the NDA.

Kapil smiled. "There were many. But my favourite is actually the one that happened in one of our senior courses. Once a Cadet came to the drill square with his belt loosely fastened. The drill ustad looked at him and raised an eyebrow. The Cadet, half-terrified, said in a small voice, "Stomach ache hai ustad." The ustad, without breaking stride, replied, "Stomach ek ho yah do, Belt tight kyon nahin hain?"

We all laughed.

"But it was not always so bad. We did enjoy a lot. The people who were with us stuck around no matter what. You know, NDA really teaches you how to live. You struggle, you fight, but you also have fun. That is the best part."

We were keen to understand how the bond developed between him and his batchmates.

"You mean our course-mates," corrected Kapil. "Here, for the first 5 terms, you are doing everything together. You only start specialising in the sixth term. The bond between course-mates is deep. We can call our mates at 1 or 2 at night, and they will still pick up their phones."

"We train together, stay together, eat together, fight together, and if we are lucky, we will also die together. Course-mates can do anything for each other."

It was around 12 noon when we realised our meeting was coming to an end. Kapil decided to walk us to the parking lot. A group of cadets were marching to their squadron in a 2x2 formation. They greeted Kapil with a full-throated 'Jaihind Saab' (a salutation used in the armed forces when junior soldiers salute their seniors) without pausing or breaking stride. It happened as if they were anticipating Kapil's presence.

We reached the parking lot. Kapil bid us goodbye and moved swiftly towards the officers' mess. As we were pulling out of the parking, we saw an ustad barking orders at a group of cadets. The ustad had a baton and was swinging it wildly above the young men, who were crawling with guns. The cadets crawled without pausing or showing any signs of fatigue, even though their skins were clearly reddened under the scorching heat.

"Forged in fire," was the thought that came to our minds as we slowly drove away.

Author's note: We travelled to the NDA many times, as a part of the research for this book. We visited the cadets' mess, the squadrons, the training grounds, and other parts of the NDA. We interacted with young cadets, who came from different parts of India, from all sections of society. We asked them about their aspirations and dreams for their future. They spoke with clarity, poise, and confidence. They gladly accepted the leadership responsibilities that they will carry on their young shoulders in the years to come. The future of our country's armed forces is in capable hands.

Chapter 3
The Bal is in Our 'Kot'

*Amidst all leadership quotes, lessons, and slogans, one forgets a leader needs to bring deep **competence** and knowledge to the table. Leaders need to know the subject matter that their teams operate in better than the team members themselves. And in high-performing teams, incompetent leaders get exposed early. This story is about a top-notch squadron of the Indian Air Force that participated in the Balakot bombings of 2019. And their exceptional leader who led a team of highly skilled Air Force pilots, simply by being the best amongst them.*

Wing Commander Shourya Bajaj clicked the stopwatch as soon as he huffed and puffed through the front gate of his housing quarters. The guard shot up from his seat the moment Saab stormed in like a gust of wind, but Shourya was concentrating too hard to notice it. Panting, he checked the time. Yes! he was 5 seconds faster today. In his line of work, time was everything. Time, Shourya thought and recalled what his Commanding Officer had once said, "Time is like the red cloth in a game of tug-and-war. Whoever's side it's on, wins the game." This had made him ponder and that's when he realised that his greatest enemy were not the Pakistanis or Chinese, but "time".

Since that day, Shourya did everything by the clock, as if he wanted to own time. He walked faster, much to the annoyance of his wife, Nikita, ate within a specific time limit, and even monitored his daily movements and exercise patterns. Time was everything for him.

Shourya took a quick shower and sat at the breakfast table with a healthy serving of omelette, toast, oatmeal, and a cup of steaming filter coffee. Nikita was in the gym and would not come back in the next hour or so. He loved these quiet mornings when he had time to relax and have a good meal. He switched on the TV and quickly navigated to the news channels. The newspaper would arrive later, but he could not wait for it. On most days, he got his daily dose of news from the TV or Twitter (now X). Shourya chuckled. News travelled faster on the microblogging platform than anywhere else.

As he paused at his favourite news channel, a wide smile spread across his face. The headline flashed: One year anniversary of Balakot. Has anything changed?

Shourya raised his cup and answered, "Everything!" as his mind went spiralling back to the day it all happened.

On 14th February 2019, Shourya drove into the Gwalior Air Base, where he had been posted after being commissioned as a fighter pilot, with an extra dose of excitement. It was Valentine's Day, and he had promised Nikita a sumptuous dinner at the Taj Ushakiran, Gwalior's only 5-star hotel. But she didn't know about the pendant waiting for her in the tray that the waiters would serve her. He had a feeling it was going to be a good day.

After the day's briefing, he left for the morning flying sortie with a senior, both flying their respective fighter aircraft. Usually, in the afternoon, he went back home, had a nice lunch, and on some days even caught up on a power nap before heading back to the base for the evening drills. But that day, he decided to stay back with a couple of other guys. After a late lunch, they got busy at the pool table. Shourya was so busy that he did not notice the men leaving the table. When he realised it, the news came floating in his ear ".... CRPF soldiers dead in Pulwama ... deadliest terror strike since 26/11 ...." He left the pool table and joined the others near the TV set. With every new piece of information, his blood started boiling. An SUV loaded with 300 kilograms of explosives rammed into the convoy, killing 40 innocent CRPF personnel. He didn't remember much else about that day except one thing – Badla. Revenge.

Over the next few days, there was a hushed silence around the Air Force base, as if everyone were afraid of speaking about it aloud. Shourya knew this was the silence before the storm, and everyone kept mum because they did not want to jinx it. But it was hard not to talk about it. Some of them did mention "going there and dropping a few bombs," but it was mostly in hushed tones. But little did they know then that a plan was already in motion and would only be revealed to them when the time was right.

The right time finally came on 25th February when select fighter pilots from all three fighter squadrons, that are a part of the Gwalior base, were summoned for a sudden meeting. Shourya was lucky enough to be a part of it because he was rated as an ace fighter pilot and was sufficiently senior in the squadron. He also proved his leadership mettle many times and was currently leading a flight of four fighters. In the Air Force, only the best performers in air fighting tactics and competence were selected, and he was one of them. He topped every exam he ever sat for and came first in every sport he participated in. He got the best scores in the flight simulations. All Shourya ever wanted to do in life was fly a fighter jet and be known as a "fighter pilot's fighter pilot." Someone that even the best fighter jocks in the Air Force looked up to.

The brief was quick and simple. They would fly as one single unit, bomb Balakot, and come back.

"But why Balakot?" asked one of his colleagues.

The Commanding Officer pointed at a place on the map. "Balakot is the perfect place because it is away from the populated areas, and so no civilians will get hurt. It's a place in Khyber Pakhtunkhwa, an area that falls in Pakistani territory. And since we already know that the training camps of Jaish-e-Mohammed are in Balakot, we know our targets as well. Our intelligence also suggests that anticipating an Indian retaliation, Jaish has moved all their terrorists away from camps near the Indian border to Balakot. They assume we will never hit it as it is deep in Pakistani territory, almost near the Pakistan-Afghan border."

Finally, on 26th February 2019, the IAF (Indian Air Force) undertook one of the most offensive attacks by the Indian forces in recent years. They wanted to give a befitting reply on Pakistani soil and teach them what it felt like to lose in their own backyard.

Shourya was agitated, but he kept it to himself. He went back to every manoeuvre, every single move, and every sortie he did. When he joined the squadron as a youngster, even before he could touch an aircraft, he undertook some serious flight simulations where each test flight and scenario were scrutinised and critiqued every single day. He then, under the watchful eyes of an instructor, applied the simulator learnings in the real aircraft. He and his pilots strived for perfection because up there, in the sky, everything could change in a matter of seconds. It's like Usain Bolt spending hours training every day just to conquer a few seconds on the track.

Time. The timing was important. Even the place and time of the attack were carefully chosen.

At 2:00 AM in the morning, they began marching towards their Mirages. Shourya clearly remembers it was a cool night with the breeze gently blowing on their faces. Usually, Nikita slept when he had a night sortie, but that night, she was awake looking at the night sky. She knew something was up but did not know what. And to maintain operational secrecy, Shourya could not tell her where he was going. The country, however, slept peacefully, and that is how the IAF wanted it to be.

In front of them, the Mirage 2000 jets stood in quiet attention, almost as if they were alive, patiently waiting for their pilots to become one with them. These French-origin fighter jets powered by a single engine are known worldwide for their high manoeuvreability, advanced avionics, and high-speed capabilities. They have been used in various combat operations, including air-to-air combat and air-to-ground attacks. It was incredible how fast these beasts moved at Mach 2.2 or approximately 2,336 kmph. The 14.36 m long fourth-generation fighter jets that Shourya was about to fly were the same ones used in the Kargil War. It had nine weapon hardpoints and could carry a single 20-kiloton nuclear bomb if required.

They were going to use two kinds of bombs called standoff weapons. These bombs are released approximately 80-100 km from the target, and they automatically find their targets using GPS and other guidance mechanisms.

The best part about standoff weapons was that the pilot could keep his distance and still get the desired result.

The Mirage Shourya was flying carried a bomb called Spice 2000. The coordinates are fed, and once released, the glide scope of the bomb searches and hits the target. It won't hit anything else other than the coordinates that have been inputted. The other type of bomb they were going to use was called the Crystal Maze. In this case, the pilot controls the trajectory of the bomb, just like a remote-controlled car, as opposed to the Spice 2000.

Shourya was shocked when one of his seniors told him that each weapon cost about 2-3 crores. But then it made sense. *Our government did not spare any expense for the security of its countrymen,* he thought as he strode towards his machine.

Shourya clasped his helmet and climbed inside the cockpit. As soon as he slid the canopy shut, a silence engulfed him. For a few seconds, he sat there and closed his eyes, as if meditating. It was his ritual. He was becoming one with his machine because once he started flying, his machine's success was his success, and vice versa.

The Mirages stood in a single line, waiting for instructions. The plan was to send a strike force consisting of about 16 jets across 3 squadrons to Balakot. Out of these, 12 carried bombs while the other 4 were escorts.

If the Pakistani jets somehow attacked them, then the 4 escorts would protect the 12 from harm. The 16 fighter jets would find pockets where there was no radar coverage and use them to enter the enemy territory.

But the Air Force had another trick up its sleeve, and that's where India's most feared fighter, the Sukhoi-30 (Su-30), came into the picture. Around 15-30 Su-30s were going to create a distraction at specific locations while flying towards Pakistan. These aircraft would fly at the radar level, and while the Pakistani jets were responding to them, the main strike package of 16 Mirages would hit the desired camps. It was just like a good magic trick. While the audience is distracted, the magician has already performed the trick.

After receiving instructions on his headset, Shourya revved up the engine. When the orders came, the jets moved in a single file and in one swift motion zoomed out at breakneck speed from the Gwalior Air Base. They travelled towards the border and quickly refuelled using the IL 76 midair refuelling tankers before crossing into Pakistan. Once he was close to the border, Shourya could think of nothing else except completing the task at hand. It's as if someone had flicked a switch and shut down the part of his brain that stored all worldly activities.

At approximately 3:45 AM, they reached their destination, and once they were within 80 km from the targeted locations, they dropped their bombs. Recognising that they were deep in enemy territory, Shourya, and his team did not wait to see the outcome because they were confident that the bombs had found their targets, which was later confirmed by satellite images and on the ground intelligence. Two buildings, one a hostel where a bunch of Jihadi students were sleeping and the other a guest house for the instructors were hit, instantly killing an estimated 300-350 Jihadis, including the senior trainers. At the time, he did not feel anything because completing the mission without any goof-ups was the top priority. Within a few minutes of the bombing, the fighter jets flew back to the base. He clearly remembers the moment when he got down from the jet. There was jubilation, and people cheered, whistled, and celebrated like it was a New Year's party. As they walked back for the debriefing, the sky slowly turned orange. The darkness was disappearing, the light was getting stronger. It was a new dawn.

The soothing notes of his phone's ringtone brought him back to the present. Time to go to work. When Shourya arrived at the air base, he was greeted with a warm smile by Havaldar Khadoos, the strict guard at the entrance. He earned the name because he never smiled. At least Shourya had never seen him do so, until today. Even Khadoos remembered that this day, a year ago, the warriors of the Gwalior airbase made history.

Some days Shourya wondered how life would have been if he had not selected the Air Force in his NDA application form. Perhaps, he would have joined the Army and made good-natured jokes about the apparently cushy life the Air Force officers had compared to their Army brethren. His NDA course-mates still joked with him, asking how life was in the 'Chair Force', a reference to how most Air Force officers fought their wars while sitting, as opposed to the Army folks, especially in the infantry and armoured corps, who were always on their feet, serving in extreme heat or freezing cold. One of his course-mates, an Army man, had shown him a video where a soldier tried to fry an egg on the turret of a tank somewhere in the deserts of Rajasthan. It took some time, but eventually, the egg did fry. He also knew the mental pressure that submarine sailors went through when they sailed for a mission. For days, they would be stranded in enemy territory, and any wrong step could be seen as an act of war.

But Shourya would never trade the life he had with the one that his course-mates led. The thrill of operating at the cutting edge of technology and making decisions at the speed of sound cannot be compared to anything else.

After the briefing, Shourya changed into his flight overalls and drove slowly toward the hangars where his squadron was based. If there was anything he disliked about the Air Force, then it was the slow drive to the hangars. What an irony! In the air, they travelled at the speed of sound - over 1,200 kmph or over 3 km every second - and here he could not drive over the 30 kmph speed limit, which was strictly enforced for all vehicles driven within the Air Force station.

Near the hangar, he met Satty and Krish. "Satty, you do remember where the controls are now, right?" Shourya asked as they shook hands. Krish broke into wild laughter. Now Shourya joined in while Satty's face went red with embarrassment.

Last week, the three of them had caught up for a couple of drinks at Shourya's place. Satty and Krish flew Mig 21s, the type that Wing Commander Abhinandan had used to bring down an F-16. It's a notoriously difficult aircraft to fly because of its aerodynamics, but the Air Force had some of the best pilots to fly them. As they were talking, sipping their drinks, Satty suddenly said in all seriousness, "Dude, I had a horrible nightmare the other day. I was part of the ORP at the base, and suddenly the alarm went off."

The ORP or Operational Readiness Platform is a fully fuelled and armed fighter jet along with a pilot, that was kept ready to launch and intercept any suspicious aircraft.

The fighter must be airborne within 5 minutes of an alarm being sounded.

Satty continued. "So, I rushed to the aircraft, got in, and quickly initiated the start-up procedure. Everything was set, and all I had to do was to press the start button. But then ... then I could not remember where the start button was. The control tower was screaming into the radio, and my crew Chief was looking at me all worried, but I was frozen. I woke up sweating and could not go back to sleep the whole night."

They were laughing now, but Shourya later admitted that a chill had run down his spine and hoped that none of them faced a nightmare like that in real-life.

As he walked into the crew room of the squadron, Shourya looked at a poster that one of the younger fighter jocks had pasted on the wall, 'The difference between God and a fighter pilot is that God does not think he is a fighter pilot'. Shourya smirked. Perhaps he and his mates should permit themselves a bit of arrogance as they conquered the skies and their enemies every day and night.

Author's note: Wing Commander Shourya (name changed on request) continues to serve in the Air Force. Since the Balakot mission is still classified, Shourya refused to divulge any specific details about the mission. He encouraged us to refer to public sources. He instead spoke about his feelings leading up to the mission, life in the squadron and what motivates him. The authors weaved the public non-confidential information on the Balakot mission into Shourya's story. He still enjoys his time in the air and is the first port of call for all the young pilots who join the squadron. They all look up to him as a fighter pilot's fighter pilot. The title of this story, 'The Bal is in our Kot' has been borrowed from a plaque in the crew room of the squadron at Gwalior, an acknowledgement of the successful mission the squadron led a year ago. The authors felt that it was an apt way to start the fascinating story of Shourya and his air warriors.

Chapter 4
Unlimited Liability

*Having someone's back means protecting or defending someone, oftentimes by putting oneself at harm. We all want to work for leaders who have our back. Leaders who have the **moral courage** to put themselves between us and the wrath of an angry super boss or take the blame when we try and fail despite our best efforts. Leaders who pay a heavy price in their own careers and personal lives by doing the right thing. Col Pillay's legendary story has been told many times in the past. We are telling it again as a tribute to all those leaders who always had our back.*

Col. Divakaran Padma Kumar Pillay, DPK to his friends, was lost deep in thought, with his gaze fixated on a letter from Col Nautiyal (his Commanding Officer back in the day) to his father, taking a place on pride on the walls of his office amongst photos and degrees from his years of service in the Indian Army. It read:

Dear Major Pillay,

I, as the Commanding Officer of 8 GUARDS, the most decorated Battalion in the Indian Army, have the proud privilege of intimating to you of the superlative performance of your son Capt DPK Pillay in an encounter with the hardcore NSCN Cadre in Tamenglong district of Manipur State on 25 Jan 94.

He has done all of us proud and has achieved the ultimate for his men and his Battalion in an action. Despite being injured, the officer remained the most motivating and inspiring factor to see the successful completion of the operations. I have recommended him for the highest possible award in peacetime which he richly deserved.

I am enclosing all relevant documents for your information. 8 GUARDS owes a lot to his parents and shall ever remain indebted to the kind of grooming he has had on principles and values under you all.

Please accept my heartiest congratulations on his valiant action and inspiring leadership in a combat situation.

Capt DPK Pillay is fine and shall be with us again, as a "Celebrity" very soon. Kindly do not worry at all, he is being looked after and attended to by the best people.

With warm Regards,
Yours Sincerely
Col V Nautiyal
CO 8th Guards

It will soon be 30 years since that cold day when DPK's life and the lives of the inhabitants of that remote village in Manipur changed forever. DPK looked at the letter again and wondered how his father had felt. Pride for sure, as he had expressed when he finally met Pillay. But he might also have felt a small sense of irony. It, after all, was the same district, Tamenglong, where his father, as a young Captain, served in 1958. Wheels of Destiny ensured that two generations of the Pillay family, born in the southern state of Kerala, found themselves in the same Northeast district, almost 35 years apart. The journey that the senior Pillay started was given shape, direction, and a fitting conclusion by his own son.

DPK's actions on that fateful day, and his willingness to sacrifice his own life to save the lives of his fellow citizens, was what Col Nautiyal was referring to in his letter when he used the words "Principles and values". Some of those values were taught to DPK at home. And some of the principles he learnt as he passed through the hallowed halls of the National Defence Academy (NDA) and the Indian Military Academy (IMA).

The graduating batch of the Indian Military Academy (IMA) at Dehradun passes through the Chetwode hall after the completion of the passing out parade, marking the transition from a gentleman Cadet to a commissioned officer of the Indian Army. The hall is named after Field Marshal Philip Chetwode, the Commander in Chief of the Indian Army in the early 1930s. In that hall, enshrined in golden letters, is the Chetwode code. The Chetwode code, which every passing out gentleman/lady Cadet swears by, teaches young officers the fundamental tenets of leadership in the Army:

"The safety, honour, and welfare of your country come first, always and every time.

The honour, welfare, and comfort of the men you command come next.

Your own ease, comfort, and safety come last, always and every time."

As per the ethos of the Indian Army, the liability of an Army officer towards his citizens, his mission, and his soldiers is **'Unlimited'**. This means that he operates contrary to natural human instincts and is morally bound to walk into the line of fire, irrespective of personal danger that could also lead to him losing his life.

Captain DPK Pillay was initiated into the Army with the same principles. After passing out from the IMA, he was commissioned as an officer in one of India's oldest and most distinguished Battalions, 4 Guards, part of the unique Brigade of Guards regiment, the Army's first "all India" regiment. Usually, fixed regiments have soldiers from a specific region of India. The Gorkha regiment, for example, mostly comprises Gorkhas, or the Rajputana Rifles, which consists only of Jats and Rajputs. However, The Brigade of Guards has people from all over India, and hence, it became a place where DPK mingled with people from other cultures and vastly different backgrounds than his. DPK's Battalion, the legendary 4 Guards, had illustrious officers on its rolls like Field Marshal KM Cariappa, Lt Gen Thakur Nathu Singh, and Gen Himmeth Singh. It distinguished itself well in India's first war in Kashmir, defending Naushera and earning India's first PVC for a Non-Commissioned Officer Naik Yadunath Singh. 4 Guards also spearheaded the attack, crossing the Meghna River and entering Dacca in 1971. Before independence, the paltan had seen action in many campaigns from China to Africa and Europe.

After the initial training in 4 Guards, DPK was posted on cross-attachment for a period of one year with 8 Guards, a sister Battalion (paltan) of the Guards regimen. They were deployed in Operation Rhino in Assam and subsequently moved for Op Hifazat in Manipur in 1994. Manipur was a region of unrest due to the activities of the National Socialist Council of Nagaland (NSCN), a Naga nationalist separatist group operating in the NorthEast region, mostly in the Naga areas of Manipur and Nagaland. Moreover, the Kuki Naga ethnic clashes added to the level of unrest. The Indian Army was aware that the main target of the separatist group were young men who either joined them due to a lack of opportunities or, in many cases, were brainwashed and turned into insurgents.

In one such incident, Captain Pillay's CO, Col Nautiyal, received news that 4 insurgents had taken shelter at Longdi Pabram, a remote village in the Tamenglong district of Manipur. Their mission was to destroy the already meagre infrastructure, in this case, a bridge over the river Barak and the communication tower in the district. It was critical to stop them before it was too late.

Pillay was headed to the village to protect the Kuki's from Naga attacks. When the information about the insurgents was relayed to him, Pillay and his team cordoned off the village and surrounded the house where the insurgents were suspected to be hiding.

It is important to make a distinction between militancy in Kashmir and the insurgency in parts of the North-east. Militancy in Kashmir is dominated by foreign terrorists, who cross over from Pakistan and create strife in the Kashmir valley. They receive some support from the local Kashmiris. However, in the North-east, almost all the insurgents are locals, our countrymen, who picked up a gun to fight against the state. Officers like Capt. Pillay were aware of this difference and were careful to avoid and limit collateral damage.

The peace of the dawn was shattered by firing by Havildar Madan from DPK's team, who engaged an insurgent who was fleeing the cordon. DPK reached the place where the firing took place. After his repeated calls to the house occupants to surrender went unanswered, Capt. Pillay decided to make a forced entry into the house. As the door was forced open, the insurgents fired using AK-47 rifles. Since the Captain was the first one to enter the house, he got shot. One bullet had found his chest and the two others, his arm. In the melee, the insurgents tossed a grenade, which exploded near Captn Pillay's foot. DPK's buddy, Guardsman Hardeo Singh pulled him back, and a gunfight ensued. The encounter raged for over 90 minutes and finally ended when the Captain brought out the rocket launcher and threatened to blow up the place. The insurgents knew their game was up. Their commander was dead, two insurgents surrendered, and one insurgent escaped. All through the gunfight, DPK, though grievously injured, directed and motivated his soldiers till the operation concluded.

As they combed through the house, Captn Pillay was shocked to find that two little children, a girl and a boy, were in the house and were caught in the crossfire. Dingamang Pamei, the 6-year-old boy, had been shot in the leg while his sister, Masebiliu Thaimei, had been shot in the stomach. With a sinking feeling, Captain Pillay realised that the children were hit by the bullets fired by his soldiers. He felt sick at the thought that armed men, in this case, the insurgents, would use innocent children as a human shield.

The scope of DPK's injuries was communicated to the Army HQ, and a helicopter was on its way to evacuate him.

However, as soon as the helicopter arrived to evacuate him, Capt. Pillay refused to go. He insisted that the children be airlifted first. It was a Cheetah, a small helicopter and

Unlimited Liability

could either carry the children or DPK at one time. On the radio, after trying to talk him out of this decision for a few minutes, his CO, Col Nautiyal, realised that he did not have a choice and instructed the helicopter pilot to evacuate the children first.

DPK's instincts told him that the kids wouldn't survive the 6-hour journey to the nearest hospital by road. Lying half-dead in the tiny village, he could only remember that his liability to save these two innocent children was **unlimited**.

By this time, DPK, who had lost a lot of blood and was fading in and out of consciousness, realised that he was running out of time. He took a promise from his soldiers that they would not harm anyone in the village, in case he did not make it out alive.

Eventually, the helicopter returned, and the unconscious Captain was evacuated. It was probably by DPK's sheer will or the prayers of the mother of the two little children, or probably both, that both he and the two children survived.

16 years later, when an Indian Army patrol visited the long-forgotten village of Longdi Pabram, they were shocked to find a small memorial to the unknown Army officer who had given his life to save the lives of two young kids.

The villagers thought that DPK had died. They tearfully narrated to the confused Army personnel the story of Capt. Pillay and his sacrifice. The story was passed along through the Army channels, and an amused DPK, now a Colonel, was told that in the villages of the Tamenglong district, he was already a ghost.

On the 8th of March 2010, Col Pillay made an emotional journey back to the village where he had nearly died. The moment he arrived at the old village, he was received as a hero. He met and hugged the mother who had prayed for her children and him in the same breath. He met the two little children, now all grown up. He also met the insurgent who admitted that he was the one who threw the grenade at him all those years ago.

He was welcomed as a member of the tribe in the village of Longdi Pabram, a rare honour. DPK realised that the root cause of the insurgency was poverty and lack of development. He used his access to the National Security Council and the Secretariat to get roads and other amenities developed in the village. These included playgrounds, water tanks, and vehicles for the villagers to quickly take their produce to the local markets. He also worked with influential friends like Dr. Devi Shetty to train the young men and women of the village as nurses and medical technicians. What started as a small batch of 25 students has now grown significantly over the years. In small incremental steps, DPK's efforts completely transformed a poor underdeveloped village. More importantly, it proved to all of us that basic human values transcend all cultures, customs, regions, and religions.

Col Pillay sighed as he put the letter back on the wall in his office. The people of Longdi Pabram and he were joined together by some unknown force of destiny. All those years ago, he thought he was following his principles and doing his duty. But he was also sowing the seeds that would one day uplift an entire village and a district. Seeds that would also break the unending cycle of violence that consumes different parts of the world caught in the throes of conflict. The Pillay's were from Kannur, Kerala. But they truly belonged to Longdi Pabram, Tamenglong district, Manipur.

Author's note: Col DPK Pillay SC (retd.) served with distinction in the Indian Army and later in the Ministry of Defence and the National Security Council (NSC). He also worked with the International Committee for the Red Cross, the custodian of the Geneva Conventions which he upheld when he protected the children and put their lives first. He retired from the Indian Army and currently works as a research fellow, at the Manohar Parrikar Institute of Defence Studies and Analyses. He is a prolific writer, researcher and an active participant in all areas related to defence and social studies. He continues to be a part of the lives of the people of Longdi Pabram. The little girl, Masebiliu Thaimei, is now happily married and has children of her own. Her brother, Dingamang Pamei, is married and works as a manager in a private sector bank in Imphal.

Chapter 5
Fortune Favours the Brave

*Great leaders like Dwight Eisenhower and Napoleon Bonaparte were known to say that they preferred lucky Generals to Generals who were just good or smart. While analysing success, we underplay the role that **luck, or good fortune**, might have played. Great leaders recognise the small breaks that occasionally come their way through sheer luck and convert these breaks into catalysts for great wins. This story talks about leaders who brought superlative leadership and raw courage to the table but caught a lucky break that delivered India her most famous victory during the 1971 Bangladesh war.*

There was that feeling again in the pit of his stomach as he tightly grabbed the controls of his helicopter. Flight Lieutenant Pushp Vaid smiled. Flying a dangerous mission in the dead of the night, deep into enemy territory, would terrify most people. But Flt LT Vaid was different. He was not afraid. Excitement, that was what he was feeling deep inside. This was a rare opportunity to run a mission at night, something that had not been done before. Flt LT Vaid, Pushp to his friends, was keen to find out what the night held. The success of this night-time mission could be a significant force multiplier for the 1971 Bangladesh war effort. As he looked towards his co-pilot, Flying Officer BLK Reddy, he thought back to the sequence of events that got them to undertake this mission.

His helicopter unit, the 105 HU, was assigned to the IV Corps, as part of the Eastern command of the Indian Army. The IV Corps was Commanded by the legendary General Sagat Singh. General Sagat Singh, as a Brigadier, helped the Army liberate Goa in 1961 when the state was still under the control of the Portuguese. He continued his fearless leadership during further stints in the Mizo hills in 1967 and gave the Chinese a bloody nose at Nathu la later that year.

As the 1971 war against Bangladesh began, General Singh was given the task of advancing into Bangladesh from Tripura and, if possible, capturing the town of Chittagong. He was instructed to stay east of the mighty Meghna River, which provided some protection to Dhaka (Dacca in those days) from any Army advancing towards it. He was told that he was not to cross the Meghna River. However, General Singh was not satisfied with these orders. He realised that the entire war could be shortened significantly if they advanced towards Dhaka, avoiding large towns where the bulk of the Pakistani Army was stationed. Standing between him and his daring plan to advance towards Dhaka, was a Pakistani Brigade stationed in the town of Sylhet, a town that was about 250 kms from Dhaka. He had to somehow keep this Brigade, consisting of nearly 3000 soldiers tied down and busy so that they wouldn't be able to come to defend Dhaka when General

Singh finally made his move. And in order to keep the Pakistanis bogged down at Sylhet, General Singh conjured another bold plan of using multiple helicopter sorties to land an entire Battalion of Gurkha soldiers i.e., 800 men, right in the middle of the Pakistani formation.

That is where Pushp and his boss, Group Captain Chandan Singh were asked by General Singh to step in and help execute this plan. Both Pushp and Group Captain Chandan were keen to participate as this would have been India's first Heli-drop operation. On the 4th of December, Pushp and the other helicopter pilots were ready to take the first set of soldiers across. However, the Gurkha Battalion, 4/5 Gurkha, had just returned from another demanding operation and were being resupplied. When they reported to the helipads, it was already late afternoon and by nightfall, only half the Battalion was dropped at Sylhet. By this time, the Pakistanis were alerted to the presence of the Indian soldiers and were continuously firing at the incoming helicopters.

The Army was worried that the Gurkhas, at half strength and with very limited supplies, could be overrun by the Pakistanis at daybreak. However, Group Captain Chandan Singh was adamant they wait till dawn as the helicopters and the pilots had no experience of operating in the area under darkness. After a lot of back and forth, it was decided to send one helicopter, also called chopper in military lingo, with two pilots flying it and some supplies as a test mission to see if night sorties could be flown. As the senior pilot, Pushp volunteered for the mission. He needed a co-pilot. He walked up to the crew room, where all the other helicopter pilots were sitting. He explained the almost suicidal nature of the mission and asked for volunteers. His heart swelled with pride when he saw all the hands in the crew room go up. If he was going, then his team would want to go with him. He selected Flying Officer Reddy.

Pushp flew towards Sylhet. His chopper was loud, and he knew Pakistanis could hear him coming. He was told that the Gurkhas would light a fire in a clearing to help guide the helicopter. As he reached Sylhet, he saw the first set of tracers race towards his helicopter. Tracer bullets, popularised by Ravi Shastri during his commentary, are basically machine gun bullets that have a small charge in their base, that burns bright when they are fired. This allows the machine gunner to visually trace the path when he fires the gun at night. Unlike Hollywood and Bollywood movies, where each bullet seems to catch fire, in a real war, every fifth bullet in a machine gun is a tracer bullet. As Pushp saw the tracers aimed at him, he realised that for every tracer he saw, there were 4 more bullets coming at him that he could not see. He braced for the bullets to pierce through the thin outer skin of his chopper. Miraculously, nothing happened. They saw the small fire and moved the helicopter towards the location. Unfortunately, the Gurkha soldier who lit the fire was fired upon by the enemy and was hurt in his hand. They quickly landed and started unloading the helicopter. Pushp went around the machine and was surprised to see that not a single bullet had hit the the machine.

The unloading took less than 5 minutes, and it was time to go back, along with the soldier who was hit and needed to be evacuated for medical attention. The departure got delayed because the brave Gurkha insisted that he was okay and could easily fight the Pakistanis with only one functional hand. After the intervention of his seniors, the chopper finally took off with the angry Gurkha who was upset that he was leaving his mates behind to fight. As the chopper took off, the angry tracers followed the helicopter's path again without hitting it. Pushp was amazed that they were unscathed, but suddenly realised the reason why. It was a dark moonless night. Just as he could not see anything in the dark, the Pakistani soldiers also could not see his chopper. They were aiming at the sound of the helicopter, and by the time they fired at the sound, the helicopter had moved some distance. Ideally, the Pakistanis should have aimed and fired a bit ahead of where they thought the sound was coming from. But they didn't, and Pushp was grateful for that.

They landed back at Agartala, and Pushp confidently walked into the crew room and announced "These Pakis can't fire straight. I feel the night sorties are safer for us to do than even day sorties."

By the time dawn broke, the Indian Air Force helicopter pilots ran multiple sorties and got the entire 4/5 Gurkha Battalion, along with the necessary weapons, equipment, and food stocks on the ground to further fortify their position.

The courageous aviators kept the Gurkhas supplied throughout the course of the battle at Sylhet. Pushp personally flew over 90 sorties. Each sortie lasted about an hour. They transported over 2000 tonnes of equipment during the operation. In many cases, they loaded the helicopters far beyond what they were designed to carry. They barely had any sleep. Most of them slept for a few minutes between sorties (catnaps in Pushp's words), mainly in the helicopters when they were being loaded or serviced at the main base. They took quick bathroom breaks and wolfed down their food. They knew they were the lifeline for their Gurkha brothers back in Sylhet. They needed to go back as soon as they could, either to re-supply or evacuate battle casualties. They flew through a hail of bullets and multiple artillery and mortar attacks on the landing zones where they put down their helicopters. However, other than minor bullet holes, no helicopter got seriously hit. The Pakis just could not shoot straight.

As he flew multiple sorties, Pushp had a ring-side view of the fighting raging on the ground. On the first sortie, he briefly met the Commanding Officer of the 4/5 Gurkhas, Lt Col Arun Bhimrao Harolikar. He saw a firm determination in Col Harolikar's eyes. He also saw a bit of weariness. The 4/5 Gurkha had bravely fought two other battles at Atgam and Gazipur and emerged victorious. However, they paid a heavy price for these victories. 7 of the 18 officers of the Battalion were either wounded or martyred in those battles. They also lost about 20 other soldiers, and close to 70 soldiers were wounded. The Battalion was exhausted and short-staffed. Col Harolikar was expecting some rest and recuperation time for his men. However, they were immediately pressed into the battle at Sylhet. General Sagat Singh himself had served with and commanded a Gurkha Battalion and had deep faith in the hill warriors from Nepal. He was confident that they would achieve the difficult objective of keeping the Pakistani Brigade pinned down. Unfortunately, in addition to being tired and short-staffed, the Gurkhas were fed faulty intelligence that there was only one Pakistani Brigade on the ground. Unknown to the Indians, another Brigade had reinforced the original Brigade, taking the total to almost 6000 enemy soldiers. Moreover, there were additional Pakistani troops at the

Sylhet Garrison, taking the total number of soldiers to nearly 8000.

The Gurkhas did not know any of this. They were expecting a Brigade. They knew they were outmanned and outgunned. However, orders were orders, and they had a mission to achieve. It helped that they had some local support of a couple of hundred Mukti Bahini soldiers. Mukti Bahini was a guerrilla resistance movement of local Bangladeshis, trained by the Indians. The Bahini were fighting for the liberation of Bangladesh. The Gurkhas and Mukti Bahini dug into their positions. The wise Col Harolikar realised that being deep within the war zone surrounded by the enemy on all four sides, it would be difficult for a relief party of soldiers to break through to relieve them. He instructed his troops to carry more ammunition instead of food. He also spread the troops wide and kept changing firing positions. He smartly realised that given the multiple sorties that the Air Force had executed, the enemy would not be able to gauge the actual number of Indian troops that were on the ground.

However, on relatively flat ground, the numerically superior Pakistanis, operating at a ratio of nearly 1:15, could have easily overrun the Indian positions in a matter of days if not hours. The Gurkha troops would have fought against all odds to the last man and the last bullet. However, the major Pakistani attack that was expected never happened.

That's where **Fortune favoured the brave** men of the 4/5 Gurkha Regiment and their Mukti Bahini colleagues.

In a war zone, especially in 1971, intelligence on the ground was always unreliable and faulty. The other source of information would have been the radio bulletins from the Pakistani or Indian side that always exaggerated their victories and suppressed their losses. However, the one reliable source of truth on both sides were the BBC (British Broadcasting Corporation) radio bulletins on the war. These bulletins were surprisingly real-time and consistently accurate. However, for this battle, the BBC made a rare error. The BBC bulletin announced that the Indians had landed a Brigade at Sylhet. When the Pakistanis heard this news and verified it with hundreds of sorties and multiple firing positions, they were convinced that they were facing a full Indian Brigade. And when they saw that the leading Battalion in this Brigade were troops of the 4/5 Gurkha regiment, they lost their nerve. They had heard horror stories of the dreaded kukri (a short sword with a distinct recurve, that every Gurkha soldier carries with him) being put to good use at the battles of Atgam and Gazipur. It is said that the sight of a Gurkha with the unsheathed kukri running at the enemy, yelling the blood-curdling war cry 'Ayo Gorkhali' causes recurring nightmares for those who survive the Gurkha assault.

Lt. Col Horalikar also heard the same BBC bulletin and could not believe that this small bit of good fortune had come their way. He doubled down on the strategy of spreading his troops and giving the Pakistanis a sense that they were fighting a Brigade and not just a Battalion.

The Pakistanis used longer-range weapons like artillery and mortars to bombard what they thought were the Indian Brigade positions. Had they instead used foot soldiers, and regular infantry in large numbers to directly assault the Gurkhas, the battle would have been swiftly over. It was clear that the Pakistanis did not have the stomach to directly fight the Gurkhas man to man.

The initial Heli-drop happened on the 7th of December. The Gurkhas engaged the Sylhet-based Pakistani brigades, while the Indian Army surrounded Dhaka. General, later Field Marshal Sam Manekshaw (Sam Bahadur) gave an ultimatum to the Pakistani leadership to surrender. The surrender finally happened on the 16th of December, and nearly 90,000 Pakistani troops in Bangladesh surrendered, handing India a magnificent victory. The troops of 4/5 Gurkha held the Pakistanis at bay for nearly 9 days through sheer grit, ingenuity, and a little bit of luck. When the surrender was announced, the Pakistani Brigadier requested that the Brigadier on the Indian side accept the surrender of the Pakistani troops. By now, due to casualties suffered in the battle, the Gurkhas were reduced to less than 350 troops. The Pakistanis were surprised to see the Indian Brigadier flying in through a helicopter to accept their surrender. They were shocked to find that they were facing not a Brigade, but a Battalion, that too a Battalion that was reduced to half its strength. The Gurkhas were shocked too when they realised that they were facing off against not just a Brigade, but 2 brigades and the entire Sylhet Garrison, a total of 8000 men. If their knees went weak after hearing this, the Gurkhas did not show it.

In the history of the Indian Army, never before and never after did 3 Brigadiers, 173 officers, and nearly 8000 enemy soldiers surrender to an Indian force of only about 350 men. The efforts of bold leaders like Flight Lieutenant Pushp Vaid, Lt Col. Arun Horalikar, and the officers and men of the 105 HU and 4/5 Gurkha delivered India an impossible victory at Sylhet and hastened the fall of Dhaka.

Author's Note: Squadron Leader Push Vaid ran multiple missions during the war. After the successful Sylhet operation, the air warriors of 105 HU used the lessons learnt to help IV Corps troops cross the Meghna River and finally assault Dhaka. For his contributions at Sylhet and the Meghna operations, he was honoured with a Vir Chakra, India's third-highest wartime gallantry award. After the war ended, Squadron Leader Vaid took voluntary retirement and moved to Scotland, where he flew helicopters for oil exploration companies. He is retired and currently lives in Scotland and shared his stories with the *authors through multiple Zoom calls. His recently released book 'Mi-4's at War' details his experiences fighting the war of 1971. As a part of our research into the events at Sylhet, we also referred to a book written by the legendary Maj General Ian Cardozo, titled '1971:Stories of Grit and Glory from the Indo-Pak War', which details the Sylhet ground operation in one of the stories. Gen Cardozo was the 2nd in Command of the 4/5 Gurkha during the Sylhet operation. He lost a leg while fighting at Sylhet but did not allow the injury to impact his Army career and continued serving, eventually retiring as a Major General.*

Chapter 6
INS Resilience

*Murphy's law states that 'Anything that could go wrong will go wrong". When things don't go according to plan, good leaders don't get flustered. They are **'Resilient'** enough to consider all available options and find alternative pathways to make their missions successful. No environment in the armed forces is more unforgiving than fighting underwater. In the depths of the ocean, the Indian Navy's submarines and their sailors put their lives at risk to patrol the high seas silently, ready to use deadly force if needed to defend our homeland. This story is about one such submarine, led by an outstanding leader who remained unfazed and resilient during an extremely demanding mission.*

Bhargav sat in his tiny cabin aboard the Diesel-Electric submarine that he commanded. For a man who will be subjected to extreme stress over the next 45 days, Bhargav was outwardly very calm. He had to be. His Russian-origin submarine, almost 30 years old, was prone to frequent breakdowns and equipment failures. If he was lucky, these breakdowns would happen when he was submerged, but in the Indian territorial waters. However, most of Bhargav's luck was downright rotten and these issues happened when he was submerged in foreign territorial waters, where coming up to the surface of the ocean was not advisable.

It recently happened on his last patrol, when they were operating off the coast of a neighbouring country. Due to a failure in his navigation equipment, they strayed into the Meghna River estuary area, where the mighty Meghana river flows into the Bay of Bengal. Most submarines are designed to operate in salt water as the salinity in the water keeps the submarine afloat. However, as they strayed into the estuary which is dominated by fresh river water, the salinity levels dropped and the submarine started sinking. There was near panic in the control room, the area from which the submarine is controlled by the key officers and men. Bhargav quickly decided to adopt a procedure called Emergency Blow, where an extremely high amount of compressed air is forced into the ballast tanks of the submarine very quickly to force the submarine to the surface. However, it took ages for the submarine to react.

Bhargav's entire life became a reel and flashed in front of his eyes. Very soon his submarine would hit the bottom and become a 3,500-tonne coffin for him and his men. After what seemed to be an eternity, they started moving up and surfaced. Later, when they checked the data, they were less than a metre away from hitting the bottom. Shivers run down his spine even today when he remembers that day.

The Indian Navy's submarine force consists of about 18 submarines. Almost all are imported from Russia,

Germany, and France. The majority of these submarines are Diesel-electric attack submarines. They use large lead-acid batteries, similar to the smaller ones found inside a car, which are charged and recharged by running a diesel engine. A Diesel-electric submarine, when running on its batteries, is nearly 100% quiet and virtually undetectable and can be a significant threat to Navy surface fleets and other submarines.

However, in order for the internal combustion engine to work, oxygen needs to mix with the fuel, which is why it uses a device called a snorkel. The submarine comes to just below the ocean surface, and a tube, which is part of the snorkel, rises to the surface. The tube absorbs oxygen from the air, and the exhaust dissipates into the ocean. A typical Diesel-electric submarine's batteries last about 3 days; however, most submarine captains try to charge their batteries every day to avoid an emergency loss of power. Unfortunately, this is the time when the submarine is most vulnerable to detection by enemy anti-submarine forces.

Submarines, when fully submerged, are guided using sonars. Sound travels large distances underwater, and the submarine sonar picks it up. Experienced submarine sonar officers and onboard computers can identify the source of the sound, such as ships, aircraft, other submarines, etc. Closer to the ocean surface, submariners use a pair of periscopes to check the ocean surface while submerged.

This process is known as rising to periscope depth (PD). In fact, during a patrol, after a submarine leaves the port and submerges, it will never surface until it comes back after the patrol. It will only rise to PD, check its surroundings, use the snorkel to recharge its batteries and submerge. All these technical facts will play an important role in Commander Bhargav's story as we move forward.

Submarines are lethal, high-technology war platforms and are hence staffed with the best officers and men available in the Royal Indian Navy. Tough men like Commander Bhargav, who is a first-generation officer, joined the Navy directly from the NDA and volunteered for the submarine service—a decision that he is grateful for but also a decision that he occasionally regrets. Each of his patrols ranges from 30 to 45 days. While on patrol, he has zero contact with the outside world, except with his senior commanders, who send him periodic orders and updates.

As Bhargav looked at the orders in his hand, he realised that this would be a dangerous mission that would take the submarine from its base in the eastern port of Vizag all the way to the enemy territory on the west coast and back. Submarine mission orders are top-secret, and only the Navy leadership and the submarine Captain have access to these orders. The rest of the crew comes to know only after they set sail and have submerged. Bhargav folded the orders and put them back in the safe in his cabin, the combination of which was known only to him. His second-in-command, known in the Navy as the Executive Officer or XO for short, would now be getting the submarine ready for departure. He would also do a count of the men and ensure that everyone was onboard. As this thought crossed his mind, Bhargav heard footsteps rapidly approaching, and the door to his cabin was flung open.

His XO looked at him, panic written large on his face. "Kartar has run away, Sir. He is nowhere to be found."

Bhargav sighed. And so it starts, he thought to himself.

"What do you mean, run away?" Bhargav asked, "Have you checked the base? Maybe he is unwell."

"No, Sir. When I couldn't find him, I asked around, and one of the sentries confirmed that he saw Kartar board a cab with his bags. His phone is now switched off."

Kartar Singh was a Junior Commissioned Officer (JCO) with over 20 years of service in the Indian Navy, the bulk of which was spent in the submarine forces. He had an impeccable track record and was one of his most dependable sailors. None of this made any sense.

Bhargav looked at his XO, "Is there something else I need to know about the situation?"

The XO hesitated. "About a week ago, he came to me asking for leave. His daughter's wedding was fixed all of a sudden, and he needed to go. I refused, Sir. He was a critical part of this upcoming patrol. I felt we could not afford to lose him."

Bhargav sighed again. "And now not only have we lost him, but he will likely face court-martial and lose all his retirement benefits. That too only a couple of years away from retirement."

AWOL, or Away Without Leave, is a serious offence in the armed forces, and personnel who go AWOL could be court-martialled and dishonourably discharged without pension benefits. In some extreme cases, they can also be jailed for extended periods of time.

Had he been in Kartar's shoes, Bhargav would have petitioned the Captain directly for leave and likely got it. But Kartar was an emotional person and would have stewed with this decision before going AWOL for his only daughter's wedding.

Bhargav came to a conclusion: "Let's sail. We don't need to tell the Naval Command that we are one sailor short."

"But Sir, that is against the rules. Even if we sail now, we will be found out after we return from the patrol."

Bhargav replied, "Call it blind faith, my friend, but I have a feeling that Kartar will be back at the port as we return. If he is not, then I will face the consequences. Let's just show him on leave. This is my decision, and it is final."

Thus, with a heavy heart and one sailor short, the submarine and her brave sailors set sail away from the port and slowly slipped under the dark waters of the Bay of Bengal.

From experience, Bhargav knew typical crew behaviour in the early part of the patrol. The men, separated from their families and leaving the familiarity of the sea breeze, sun, and the land, slowly become anxious. By day 10 of a patrol, tempers run high, and fights break out, for the silliest of reasons. There is a constant stream of offenders making their way to the Captain's cabin.

"He took my charting pencil away and refused to give it back, so I hit him" or, "Woh mujhe ghoor raha tha Saab - He was looking at me in an annoying manner Sir. In all fairness, I warned him once. When he didn't pay heed, I slapped him".

Even the officers cold shoulder each other, remembering fights real and imagined. Unless the fight was serious, Bhargav mostly let the crew work their anxieties out. Things usually settled down after a few days.

The men had a similar love-hate relationship with food. Unlike the movies, once the submarine gets underway, the officers and crew stow away their uniforms and switch to disposable shorts and shirts. The submarine forces get assigned the best chefs and top-class rations. In a confined space, the chef will brilliantly rustle up gourmet meals, and since the sailors don't have anything better to do, they just eat. Some sailors have been known to add 5-6 inches to their waistline in the first 20 days of a patrol. This love affair with food continues till fresh food stocks last. Then slowly the crew moves to tinned food, and in the last few days of the patrol, there is only khichadi and papad to eat for all three meals. The sailors use pickles to make the khichadi more palatable without much success. They then start hating food and slowly lose all those extra kilos that they put on. That is where disposable clothes help. Once the submarine comes back into the port, the crew is able to magically fit into their original uniforms.

It was day 12 of the patrol, and the submarine was on its way beyond the South Indian coast and slowly crossing the Indian Ocean. The fights had settled down, and the crew was beginning to operate as a single unit. As they were transiting through the Laccadive Sea off the Kanyakumari coast, the alarms suddenly started ringing. One of the valves started leaking heavily because of the sea pressure and flooded one of the engine compartments. The submarine has two diesel engines. Usually, even if a single engine is flooded, that's reason enough to scrap the mission. However, Bhargav was an experienced Captain, and his crew was resourceful. They surfaced and slowly used some of their freshwater reserves and started flushing out the seawater from the engine. It took them almost 14 hours to completely clean the engine and rid it of all the saltwater. The crew took turns and executed the flushing and cleaning in the open sea. The leak was plugged, and they were well on their way.

By day 20, they crossed Mumbai, and Bhargav and crew suddenly became very careful. They were only a few hundred kilometres away from the enemy coast. Unlike the Army and the Air Force, most submarine patrols tend to enter enemy waters, simulate an attack on enemy ships, and return. Since all Navies are aware that submarines are lurking under their waters, they tend to aggressively carry out anti-submarine operations to detect enemy submarines. If detected, the submarine Captain tries to slip away. If he is unable to, then the best case is to return with a wounded ego. The worst case is to not return at all.

As they entered enemy waters, Bhargav and the team had their periscopes up, scanning the waters for enemy activity. After a few minutes, they realised that both the periscopes went dark.

Unknown to them, the submarine sailed through an oil slick, and oil covered both the periscope lenses, making them unusable. Bhargav was caught in a quandary. Without their periscopes, they were half blind. However, to make the periscopes functional again, they had to surface and physically clean the periscopes. And surfacing meant risking detection. Bhargav did not have an option. After scanning the seas and potential threats, Bhargav surfaced the submarine, and a couple of sailors climbed up to the periscopes and quickly cleaned the lenses. It took 20 harrowing minutes, with Bhargav worrying that an enemy aircraft could come and detect them at any time. Thankfully, nothing of that sort happened, and they submerged after the cleaning was done. Or so Bhargav and the crew thought.

Typically, a Diesel-electric submarine's batteries need to be charged once every day using the snorkel. Mostly the snorkel activation and battery charging were done at night to reduce the chances of someone visually spotting the shape of a submarine just below the ocean surface. Moreover, since Bhargav's submarine was old, and the batteries had gone through multiple charge cycles, they lasted a little less than three days. Bhargav was aware of that, and after every charge cycle, he proactively planned for the next cycle. That meant doing a continuous surface scan with the sonar and the periscope while they were at periscope depth to check if there were any enemy ships and aircraft flying in the area where they were operating.

When Bhargav pushed the periscope up to check the surface, what he saw made his blood run cold. He could distinctly see the flashing lights of an aircraft patrolling the area where they were operating. The sonar soon confirmed that the aircraft was an enemy anti-submarine aircraft. A few miles from his position, the submarine's sonar could also hear enemy Navy vessels looking for something in the water. Given the pattern that the ships and the aircraft were following, it was clear to Bhargav that they were searching for his submarine. The 20-minute periscope cleaning exercise probably had exposed the presence of the submarine to the enemy radar. They knew he was there. They did not know where exactly he was and were desperately searching for the submarine.

Bhargav had no way of recharging his batteries given the present situation. At night, the ocean temperature was lower than the temperature of the surrounding air. If he managed to slip a little distance away and used his snorkel to charge his batteries, the hot engine exhaust that is vented into the ocean would immediately change the temperature of the surrounding water. The sensitive infrared sensors in the orbiting aircraft will at once catch the temperature change, and he would be exposed.

Bhargav immediately ordered the crew to conserve energy in the submarine and passed a 'quiet state order'. All non-essential systems were shut down. The crew, already surviving in cramped, uncomfortable conditions, had to endure further hardships. They also were asked to rest or sleep. This was done to ensure that they did not exert much and used less oxygen. But no one complained. Bhargav had to make the batteries last as long as he possibly could, as he tried to get out of this sticky situation. His options were limited. He did not have enough power in his batteries to move away from the area. He either had to manage to recharge his batteries or get caught. They kept constant watch on the proceedings, but the enemy was relentless.

Almost 30 hours had passed, but Bhargav and his crew did not get any opportunities to get the snorkel up. The sonar room usually recorded the proceedings continuously. At his wit's end, Bhargav realised that he needed to do something different. He went back to the cabin and started looking at the search patterns of the anti-submarine aircraft. He noticed that the aircraft coverage increased towards the evening and peaked in the middle of the night. And started easing up as the dawn broke. And as he further studied the patterns, Bhargav smiled.

Between 12 noon and 4 PM, there was literally zero coverage over his area. He realised that the pilots flying the aircraft were also human and needed rest. And invariably took a break post-lunch, probably a quick siesta before getting back to searching the seas.

"I should use this incident to make fun of my IAF course-mates," Bharghav thought as he looked at the search patterns.

Conventional logic says that submarines do not charge their batteries during the daytime. All alone in his cabin, Bhargav laughed hard, partly out of relief. Time to throw convention out of the window. He went back to the control room. The atmosphere was very tense. They probably had only 2-3 hours of charge left. When Bhargav shared his plan, initially the XO thought he had lost his mind. But the Captain prevailed. Against all odds, the submarine surfaced at 12 noon, in the middle of the day, and charged its batteries. And since this was done when the sun was shining bright, the temperature difference between the ocean surface and the surrounding air was not a lot.

They stayed in enemy waters for over 10 days and charged their batteries right under the nose of the enemy, who probably were surprised and frustrated that they were not able to find the submarine that they knew was somewhere in the depths of the ocean beneath them.

After a very successful patrol, the submarine left the enemy coast, and after getting resupplied at Goa, made an uneventful transit towards India's east coast. As they surfaced and pulled into the Vizag Naval base, Bhargav fought back tears when he saw a solitary figure in full Naval dress uniform, standing ramrod straight near the pier where the submarine was supposed to dock. Kartar Singh, the proud sailor and father, came back to face the consequences of his actions. As always, Bhargav's crew, even though they occasionally messed up, never let him down.

The submarine docked, and the men slowly got off onto the pier. All of them fit perfectly into their original Navy uniforms. All of them except Sub-Lieutenant Kishore. It was the young Lieutenant's first patrol. And no one knew that he loved Khichadi. Unfortunately, he did not lose all those extra inches and could not fit into his original uniform. He had to get off the submarine in his disposable dress, much to his embarrassment and some good-natured ribbing from his fellow officers.

Bhargav got onto the pier and turned back to look lovingly at his submarine. She was old, and broke down constantly, but patrol after patrol, she got him and his men safely back home. She was the epitome of 'Resilience', overcoming difficult situations but never giving up. Out of deep respect, Bhargav turned to attention and gave her a smart, sharp salute. And if she could, she too would have saluted her Captain back. After all, 'Resilience' went both ways.

Author's Note: Commander Bhargav served with distinction and got the rare opportunity to command multiple submarines over an extended command period. Over multiple sit-downs with the authors, he patiently explained the submarine world, helping demystify and simplify the complex area that submarine warfare is. He has now left the Navy and works in the private sector.

Chapter 7
Thappad se Dar Nahi Lagta

*Occasionally the other guy wins. Sometimes because he had better luck. Or sometimes because he was better than you. A leader cannot be a sore loser. He acknowledges the loss, analyses what went wrong, and learns from his mistakes. The thappad story talks about an earnest young officer and the first steps in his journey to become a better and more mature leader. Along the way, he acquired a **sense of humour** and the ability to laugh at his mistakes.*

Colonel Sanjay Sharma looked across the table at the man he was having coffee with. Lt Col Amitabh Suri was passionately talking about the Olympic games' performance of the Indian wrestlers. That was the thing about Amitabh. He was generally intense and passionate about everything.

Colonel Sanjay thought back to all those years when he first met Amitabh. Col Sanjay was then a Major and posted as a Company Commander of the Bravo Company of his Rashtriya Rifles Battalion. He was serving in the Anantnag district, one of the most beautiful places in the Kashmir valley. The Anantnag Plain, located in the central part of the district, is surrounded by high mountains and is irrigated by several rivers, making it a highly productive agricultural region. Sanjay and his soldiers would often walk through lush fields of rice, maize, wheat, and fruits such as apples, apricots, and almonds. The Wular and Manasbal lakes were equally captivating, and on clear days one could see the reflection of the sky and the surrounding mountains . But lurking just behind all that beauty was the ugly face of terror. Anantnag was a hotbed of terrorism, and it was the job of Sanjay and his troops to maintain peace within the villages of Anantnag.

After an intense year-long tenure as a Company Commander, Sanjay was getting ready to go back home on leave for a short break. When company commanders go on leave, the command of their company is temporarily passed on to another officer. Since there is a shortage of infantry officers in the field, sometimes the command is handed over to the officers of the so-called support arms of the Army like the Signals Corps or the Army Service Corps (ASC).

Amitabh was the ASC officer who was deputed to take over the command of the company from Sanjay. The ASC is a crucial group that helps with important logistics and supply functions of the entire Indian Army. Given the criticality of what they do, ASC officers are usually deputed with frontline Army regiments for them to understand and appreciate the needs and operations of these frontline units.

Typically, when company commanders go on leave, their instruction to their replacement is simple, "Keep the lights on, do basic patrolling, but don't get yourself and the men into any trouble. If you gather any intel, pass it along to me when I return and take charge again."

That's exactly what Sanjay told Capt. Amitabh Suri when he took over. And Sanjay thought his message was simple, direct, and well-understood. He was wrong.

Amitabh was young, passionate, and restless. He saw his brief command of the Bravo Company as his opportunity to make a mark. And he was not going to let this opportunity go. After Sanjay left, he immediately looked at his Area of Operations (AOR). He realised that Sanjay would have covered all the major villages. He started looking for smaller villages, which might have been skipped and promptly found a small village about 15 km away from his camp that was not covered by the frequent patrolling of the company. He called over the company's senior JCO (Junior commissioned officer).

"Saab, any reason why we skipped patrolling this village."

The JCO looked at his temporary Company Commander curiously "It's a small village Saab, and we never received any adverse intel here. Also, we have not had any incidents in this village. No terror attacks, no robberies, nothing. Kya Iraada hai Saab? What are you thinking Sir?"

"I think we should pay this village a visit," Amitabh said.

The JCO was confused "But Saab, like I just said, it's a quiet village and we have had no trouble. And anyway, Sanjay Saab has asked us to lay low."

Amitabh gave his JCO a sharp look "But Sanjay Saab is currently not in command, I am. Get a small party ready."

Amitabh, his JCO, and a 10-member team walked into the village and started interacting with the locals, who seemed surprised to see an Indian Army patrol. It was a small village, a row of 20 odd houses on each side of the single road that neatly divided the village into two equal halves. There was a small masjid and a tiny village market to help meet the basic needs of the villagers.

Soon, the news that the Army was in the area spread like wildfire. Usually, villagers enjoy being left alone and the presence of the Army inside the village meant trouble. The uneasiness among the villagers was palpable, and Amitabh knew that his presence might ruffle some feathers. It would be interesting to see what came out of it.

It was a short patrol, and the team went back to their camp. Nothing happened for a couple of days. On the third day, early in the morning, his JCO walked up to him.

"Saab, there is a man from the village we visited a couple of days ago." He says, "he wants to speak to you."

A wiry man with sharp features was presented before Amitabh. He was frisked for arms or weapons, and only when the soldiers were satisfied, he was allowed to enter. Amitabh was sitting on a big rock. Some of the soldiers were preparing a small bonfire.

"Salaam Saab."

Amitabh acknowledged the greeting "Tell me, why did you want to meet me?"

The villager hesitated "Saab, you and your troops visited our village a few days ago. This was the first time that the Army came to our village, and some of us are pretty shaken."

"Why are you shaken?" Amitabh asked him, "If you are living a normal life, then you have no reason to be afraid."

"Saab, most of us are living normal lives." The villager responded. Again hesitating.

Amitabh looked at the ID card that he held in his hand - Saleem Dar was the name of this villager who walked the entire 15 km distance from his village to meet him.

"Tell me more," Amitabh said in an encouraging tone.

Saleem looked around as if he was expecting hidden eavesdroppers to listen to their conversation.

"We have a militant who is hiding in the village, Saab."

Amitabh kept his expression neutral. But his heart leaped with joy.

"*Jackpot.*" He thought "*My first patrol and I already have a potential informant and the opportunity to locate a possible militant.*"

"I can show you the location of the house where he is, Saab. You can then go arrest him." Saleem paused, "And Saab, I heard that the Army gives money to us for any information that we give."

"We do," Amitabh responded. "If the information is accurate, then we can give about Rs 50,000."

Saleem's eyes lit up.

"But tell me, Saleem, is money the only reason why you are willing to share this information?"

Saleem's expression turned serious. "No, Saab. We were living peacefully all this while. We went about our daily lives, and the Army left us alone. But this one guy, who was a small farmer like me, went to Srinagar for a few weeks to visit family. And he came back with a weapon and dreams of a free Kashmir. From that day, I personally was living in dread that the Army might come knocking one day. That day finally came. My village will stay peaceful only if this fellow goes.."

Amitabh was impatient and wanted to strike while the iron was hot.

"Listen, Saleem. Enough talk. Let's do a deal. I can get a team together very soon. Let's go to the village. You point the house to me; we do the operation and catch the militant. And you can have your money. How does that sound?"

Saleem thought about it. "Sounds good, Saab. I have just one request. Most of the villagers know me well, and some of them have seen me leaving the village this morning. I will take you to the village outskirts and point the house to you. Then I will slip into the village. When you enter, I will challenge you, and I want you to slap me hard in front of the entire village. And then in public, ask me to buzz off. I will run away, Saab. That way, no one in the village will suspect me. After all, I have to live with these people."

Amitabh thought about it. Saleem's plan was a tad dramatic. But he also recognised that as a poor farmer who just wanted to live in peace, Saleem had taken a big risk by coming to the Army and was justified in taking these precautions.

"And, Saab, could you please give me the money when I point out the house to you? I don't want to be seen with you at any place after the operation is over. Everyone will be very suspicious. I don't want to come to this camp either."

"Don't worry, Saleem," Amitabh responded. "I will hand over the money to you as soon as you point out the house to me. Now go wait outside; these soldiers will get you a cup of tea. We will get ready to leave in 30 minutes."

Amitabh pointedly ignored his JCO's disapproving looks. It was true that he was breaking well-established procedures by trusting this villager. But he had just 20 days to prove himself and, in any case, you cannot make an omelette without breaking some eggs.

The biggest risk of moving this fast was that the villager could be leading him and his men into an ambush. But Amitabh had a way to plan for that. First, he will keep Saleem with him all the time. Whoever is planning to ambush him and his team, will think twice when they see the villager with them. Militants cannot afford to hurt the locals who provide them with support and shelter. Second, they will move on foot, in small groups and use different unpredictable routes. When they get to the village and lay the cordon, they will be on their toes, and it was a small village with fewer places for an ambush party to hide.

At 8 AM in the morning, the Bravo Company soldiers, commanded by Capt. Amitabh Suri accompanied by Saleem, left for the village. They reached the village outskirts by noon.

Saleem pointed out to a small single-story slightly dilapidated house which was close to the village market.

"I think he is alone, Saab. His wife and kids have gone to her mother's house in Banihal, about 40 kilometres from here. He probably has worked in the fields and should be resting in the house. That's what most of the villagers do at noon."

By this time, Amitabh had made an outer cordon of troops that tightly sealed the perimeter of the village. He planned to get an inner cordon organised and then lead the main raiding party of the troops along with the JCO to hit the house.

"Here, Saleem, take the money that we promised." Amitabh handed over the small bundle of 1000 rupee notes.

"Shukriya, Saab," Saleem said, as he took the money without counting and stuffed the notes into his pocket. "Please don't forget the plan that we have, Saab. You should be very convincing when you slap me. Otherwise, I will get into trouble."

Saleem's paranoia was beginning to slowly irritate Amitabh. Maybe he will enjoy slapping him after all.

He and Saleem discussed the route that he would take while running away through the cordon. The soldiers on that route were instructed to let Saleem go.

They watched Saleem slowly make his way into the village and settle into one of the houses. They gave him about 10 minutes and then surrounded the house that Saleem identified.

The commotion drew nearly the entire village out. The whole place was filled with curious onlookers who suddenly realised that the Army was there to raid a house.

Amitabh used his handheld megaphone to make an announcement to the militant hiding in the village to surrender or face death. Suddenly, they heard someone shouting in rage.

'Humare quom me aake hume dara rahe hoon. Wapas jao Indian Army. Hum yeh nainsafi nahin sahenge.' You come into our village and threaten us. Go back, Indian Army. We won't tolerate this.

Amitabh turned around and saw Saleem walk towards him. His chest was puffed, and he was ready for a fight. He came closer to Amitabh and again said, 'Wapas jao, Indian Army, wapas jao.'

Amitabh bit his lips to stifle a smile. He mustered all the strength he could in his right hand and smacked Saleem across the face. The sound of that slap reverberated throughout the village. Everyone was shocked, including Amitabh. He never knew he could slap someone so hard. The villagers looked at Saleem horrified. Did he not know that no one can take panga with the Indian Army?

Amitabh pushed Salem to the ground and said, "bhaag ja saale nahin toh jaan se maar dunga! Run away, else I will kill you."

Saleem picked himself up and scampered away like a scared mouse.

Once the staged performance was over, Amitabh and his men closed in on the house that Saleem had pointed out. They positioned themselves in a firing position and made the announcement to surrender again. But there was no response.

Also, Amitabh realised that something else was off about the whole situation. Usually, in such cases, the villagers would run helter-skelter because they knew things could get ugly fast. When Amitabh looked around, he saw that the villagers were not the least bothered by their operation. A couple of old men somehow procured a hookah and were lazily smoking away, watching the scene play out with a lot of interest. It was as if a major source of underlying tension suddenly went away.

Amitabh and his team waited another 20 minutes and finally broke into the house. It was empty. There were some meagre utensils and clothes. And some provisions. But there was no weapon. And more importantly, there was no militant.

Amitabh was getting frustrated by the minute. What did all this mean? Was the militant hiding in some other house? Did Saleem get the house wrong?

He barked at one of the old men near him, "Kidhar hai militant?" Where is the militant?

The man replied, "There are no militants here anymore Saab. Looks like you got the wrong information."

"Don't lie," Amitabh screamed. "We have good information." His pot of anger and frustration boiled over, and he could not hold himself back anymore. "Saleem told me that the militant was in this house."

"Who is Saleem?" The man asked.

"The man I just slapped, who then ran away."

The villagers looked at each other surprised, and then the whole village burst out laughing.

The old man replied, "His name is not Saleem Saab. It is Rasool. And he was the militant."

Time stood still. Amitabh replayed the entire sequence of events from Saleem's visit that morning to this moment in the village. The sincere tone, the eagerness to help, the theatrics, all ensured that Amitabh got played. In hindsight, it all made sense. It was just too easy. Saleem... sorry, Rasool, skilfully exploited his desire to prove himself and his impatience with set protocol to score a resounding victory.

The JCO looked at his boss sympathetically. "Maybe we can chase him and still catch him, Saab. It has been less than an hour since he ran."

A dejected Amitabh replied, "No Saab. I think he is gone. If this is the game that he played, then he would have charted out his escape path. He probably is far away by now." As upset as Amitabh was, he also slowly developed grudging respect and admiration for this Rasool. It took guts and intellect to step into the lion's den and defeat him.

After a few days, there was a gathering of all the officers in that area. Amitabh was also present despite knowing he would be ridiculed. The other officers spared no chance at pulling his leg.

"Maine suna koi militant hamare paise leke bhag gaya? I heard a militant ran away with our money?" said one of his seniors when he was passing by. This invited fits of laughter from the other officers.

Amitabh laughed. "Sir, a lot of you have been involved in dangerous missions. Some of you have chased a militant. You, I am sure, have shot at a militant. You even might have hit a militant when he was arrested and was in chains and handcuffs. But tell me, gentlemen, how many of you have ever slapped a militant in public and lived to tell the tale?"

For a few seconds, everyone went quiet. Then they all burst out laughing and patted Amitabh.

"Looks like you are lost deep in thought, Sir?" Amitabh's question jolted Sanjay back to the present.

"Nothing much, my friend. I was thinking about our time together in Anantnag. Fun times."

"In fact, Sir, I am glad you brought it up. That is the reason why I wanted to meet you. My promotion boards have just concluded. I have been promoted to a full Colonel and will shortly get command of my own Battalion."

Sanjay got up and hugged Amitabh and slapped his back. "This is awesome news buddy. I recognise that there are fewer command positions in the ASC, compared to the infantry. You obviously have been an outstanding performer to be selected for command. I am so proud of you."

Amitabh replied. "I owe a lot of that to you, Sir. In Anantnag, after my mess up with Rasool, I honestly thought my career was over. It was your support and your positive annual evaluation that saved me."

"No, Amitabh. Your proactiveness and your never-say-never attitude are what positioned you for success."

Sanjay was not lying. In many ways, the botched Rasool operation was not Amitabh's failure, as much as it was his. The village was under his area of responsibility. If he had acted earlier, they would have got to Rasool sooner. Amitabh was inexperienced. But he asked the questions that others should have asked. Why not this village? Why only others? The post-operation story of the Rasool incident was fascinating. Now that it was known that Rasool was a militant, the Army got in touch with his family and his village elders and tried to convince him to surrender. It took almost 6 months of constant outreach and pressure. But Rasool eventually surrendered and was rehabilitated in the village. An intelligent, fearless militant was taken out of circulation without a shot being fired.

"Are you still in touch with Rasool?" Sanjay asked.

"He called me a couple of months ago," Amitabh replied. "His daughter cracked the medical entrance and will shortly be joining a medical college. He is over the moon."

Amitabh hesitated for a moment. "Sir, I have been meaning to ask you for a long time but was too embarrassed. Did we ever get those 50,000 rupees back from Rasool."

Sanjay smiled. "No. We let him keep it. We all felt that he had truly earned it."

They both laughed.

Author's note: This story is a bit of an urban legend, essentially a work of fiction. And since this is fictional, we took a few creative liberties while bringing this story to life. The truth is that at least 2 different sources claimed that it had actually happened. However, despite our best efforts, we were unable to track the individuals involved. We recreated the story as we heard it because we thought it was powerful and had many lessons that were relevant for an aspiring leader.

Chapter 8
Turning the Tide

As a leader, you rarely get a perfect, high-functioning team. Good leaders take what they have and plug the gaps in their team's performance by upping their own game. The team delivers through the leader's sheer will and effort to succeed. However, this process creates a lot of stress for the leader and the team. Great leaders, on the other hand, organically transform their team members from average performers into consistent winners. Vijay's story characterises a similar leadership style, where he took a bunch of ragtag soldiers and transformed them into a team of outstanding performers.

Vijay gripped the plastic handle of his binoculars and looked through the lens. A tiny house in the distance enlarged in front of him. There was nothing extraordinary about it except for its inhabitants. It was his first week as the Company Commander of the Delta Company of 1RR (One Rashtriya Rifles) Regiment. He had received information that a couple of militants were taking shelter in the village. When he discovered the exact location, he immediately sprang into action. But nothing went as planned. First, it took the team almost an hour to get ready and form up. Second, the company Junior Commissioned Officer (JCO) waited for almost 45 minutes to organise, or in his case commandeer a bus that could accommodate the entire team even though the village was barely 8 Km away from their camp. After a frustrating start, when they were finally inside the bus, an immense sense of dread swept over Vijay. His pulse started racing. What if this was a trap? What if the information had been deliberately shared to lure the team out of the camp and use a roadside bomb or an IED (Improvised explosive device) to blow up the bus and the soldiers? The 20-minute bus ride was one of the most harrowing journeys Vijay had ever made.

He heaved a sigh of relief once they got to their destination unscathed. But his dread was replaced with frustration when he saw his men getting down from the bus. The clamouring of boots and weapons was unbearable, the movements of his soldiers were haphazard, and Vijay immediately knew their cover had been blown wide open. The time it had taken for them to mobilise and the noise that they made getting to the village, they looked as if they were a baraat (a wedding procession) and not one of the most respected regiments in the Indian Army. The terrorists, if any, would have already escaped. However, as a newly minted Company Commander, he had to follow the plan.

The plan was to cordon off the house and occupy every exit point. A squad would assault the house. Most likely, a gunfight would follow the forced entry, but the men were prepared. There were enough soldiers to overpower the terrorists and capture them.

Vijay quickly occupied a vantage point on a high ground to observe the operation, leaving his JCO to finish the task. But no sooner had he done so, he noticed almost 10 of his men climbed the hillock along with him, leaving 20 men to establish a cordon and carry out the operation. This exercise utterly confused him, but there was no time to voice his opinion. The team below split into two groups - the first group laid an outer cordon while the second group laid an inner cordon and started rounding up the villagers. Then they gingerly approached the target house, kicked down the door, and rushed in. Within minutes, the JCO's voice crackled on Vijay's radio. "They have run away Saab. Looks like we missed them by a whisker." Vijay thought, *Not a whisker Saab. We missed them by a mile*. Instead, he responded, "No problem Saab. Happens. Bad luck, I guess. Let's head back to the camp."

As the JCO started going through the process of arranging another bus to transport the team back to the camp, Vijay stopped him and asked, "Saab, why don't we walk back, instead of travelling by a bus?" The JCO and a couple of other soldiers exchanged perplexed looks and started complaining almost immediately. 'The journey was long by foot', 'The men were tired and hungry', 'The farmers might complain if we walked through their fields', etc. Vijay listened and calmly explained that he was the Company Commander, the senior most officer in charge and so, the group would bloody well do whatever he ordered them to do. 20 minutes later, 30 morose and extremely upset soldiers trudged through the fields towards the camp in groups of 4-6 people each. As they walked, Vijay asked his JCO a question that was nagging him for the past couple of hours, "Tell me one thing Saab, why did 10 soldiers join me on that high ground instead of joining you for the operation?"

"It was for your protection Saab," The JCO replied in a matter-of-fact tone.

Ten men were detailed for his protection! A protection that he neither needed nor did he ask for, Vijay thought and laughed out loud. This meant that there were 10 men less to support the operation. And that meant that both the outer and the inner cordons were weak and had large gaps. Even if the team found the terrorists, they could have easily escaped through the weak links in the cordon.

When they got to the camp, Vijay had lunch and lay down on his cot. As he stared at the ceiling, a flood of thoughts swept over him. He was a second-generation soldier and the first from his family to get into the NDA. After passing out, he spent a year at the IMA and was commissioned in the Mahar regiment, assigned to the 8th Battalion. Although relatively younger than its counterparts, the

Mahar regiment had already given two chiefs to the Indian Army, including the legendary Gen Krishnaswamy Sundarji who oversaw Operation Blue Star as an Army commander and as Army Chief helped eventually face-off successfully against both Pakistan and China in different operations.

Vijay's Battalion, 8 Mahar was special because it was the only Battalion in the Mahar regiment to be honoured with the Param Vir Charkra (PVC), India's highest war-time gallantry award. The PVC was awarded posthumously to Major Ramaswamy Parameswaran for outstanding bravery and brilliant leadership while fighting the LTTE militants during Operation Pawan, the Indian Army's peacekeeping mission in Sri Lanka. Every year, November 25th - the day Major Parameswaran was martyred is celebrated as the PVC day in 8 Mahar.

After about three years of service, Vijay was promoted to Captain. A couple of years later, he was asked to serve in the Kashmir valley as part of a deployment to a Rashtriya Rifles (RR)Battalion for counter-terrorist operations, as is expected from every infantry officer when he is promoted to a Captain or a Major. The RR, seconded by regular army regiments, is a specialised counter-terrorism force created by the government to tackle militancy in the Kashmir valley. Over the last 20 years, they have single-handedly dismantled the structure of militancy in the Kashmir valley, making them the best counter-terrorism force in the world.

Each RR Battalion has 4 companies named Alfa, Bravo, Charlie, and Delta. Each company, led by a Major or a senior Captain designated as Company Commander, has about 120 men under him and is responsible for a 30-40 sq km area called their Area of Responsibility (AOR). This means every intel collected and operation undertaken within its AOR is their responsibility. The mission objectives within the AOR are two-fold: first, ensure that all militants and militancy are eliminated, and second, win the hearts and minds of the local citizens.

Vijay had just taken over as the Company Commander of the Delta Company of his RR Battalion.

As day turned to dusk and eventually night, Vijay kept playing back the day's operation and his team's response in his mind. The tactical mistakes were hard to ignore. But what bothered him the most was the fact that his men hardly displayed the will to fight. Unlike the officers, the jawans spent 18 months cycling out. And the instinct for self-preservation among them was very high. They needed to be continuously motivated to push themselves harder and take the risks needed to successfully accomplish difficult missions.

As sleep slowly took over, Vijay could not help but wonder what Major Parameswaran would have thought about him and the men he led.

By the time he woke up, Vijay had his answer. Although he had never had the honour of meeting Major Parameswaran (fondly called Parry by his friends), Vijay was sure that Parry Sir would have told him "Vijay it is not what the men do, but how they are led, that makes all the difference." Parry Sir would know. On 25 November 1987, when he was returning from a search operation in Sri Lanka, his column was ambushed by a group of LTTE militants. With a cool presence of mind, he encircled the militants from the rear and attacked them, taking them completely by surprise. During the hand-to-hand combat, a militant shot him in the chest. Undaunted, Major Parameswaran snatched back the rifle from the militant and shot him dead. Gravely wounded, he continued to give orders and inspired his men to fight back till he breathed his last. The men repulsed the attack, killed 5 militants, and captured large quantities of arms and ammunition.

Vijay represented 8 Mahar, here in Kashmir. He knew that he could not let the reputation of his Battalion and the memory of his legendary unit officers like Parry Sir be tarnished by sub-par performances by his men. The few times he met his current Commanding Officer and the other company commanders of his RR unit, he could sense the low expectations that they had from the Delta Company. The company was never selected for critical missions, and they never gained the respect of the RR Battalion.

All that would soon change. Vijay started by making life uncomfortable for his men. Travelling by vehicles was banned. Vijay would make his men walk for hours at end. "*Jab tak aap apne pairo par ho, zinda ho*. As long as you move on your feet, you are alive," he would bark as he marshalled his troops along the marshy plains and hilly terrain. And every time he found someone slacking off, he would smack them in the leg with a stick and say, "*Terrorist ne tujhe maar diya*. You got killed by a terrorist." Even though Vijay's method was irritating and sometimes drew the ire of his jawans, they knew why he was doing it because at night, while having dinner, Vijay would explain that while travelling in vehicles they were sitting ducks and the terrorists could attack them anytime. But if they were marching then they were alert all the time and could easily tackle any threat.

But he did more than just bark orders. He led from the front and showed his men that he was not there to relax while everyone else did everything. Vijay shunned vehicles for missions that were 10-15 km away from the base location and instead marched with his troops. They started their journey early in the morning or at night and reached the location before the crack of dawn. Over time, everyone noticed the profound change in the soldiers. Their game was to the mark, and stamina was through the roof. The men would grind their souls out without getting tired.

The second thing Vijay did was teach his men how to be as silent as an assassin. He noticed that the equipment, especially the guns that his company used, made a lot of noise. The jawans complained a lot, and he knew it was out of his hands. They had to make peace with what they had been issued by the Indian Army. Vijay told them two things - "Towlia aur tel. Towel and oil." He showed them how with the expert use of towels and commonly found hair oil, one could use their equipment in silence. The men were amused and impressed in equal measure.

The other thing he taught his men was how to be absolutely silent on missions. Sometimes someone would cough, and while it was understandable given the cold and dry weather in the valley, he knew it would be game over in a sensitive situation. During one such occasion, someone had coughed and it gave the terrorists enough leeway to plan an escape, even though they were eventually gunned down. Vijay emphasised the fact that neither their breathing nor coughing should ever be audible while on an operation. He taught his men to cough on their sleeves and control their breathing if they felt like coughing and sneezing. After a couple of sessions, everyone in the company knew how to be as quiet as a tiger on the hunt.

The men slowly understood what it meant to be led by an officer from a PVC paltan. Their initial complaints and irritation soon turned into respect for their Company Commander. Never had they felt such energy and excitement within the company and embraced the new changes with all their heart. They started following orders to the letter, and it became obvious that under Vijay's leadership, a new Delta Company was being born.

And they slowly started seeing some early success in their AOR. Vijay had told his men to be alert about every small issue inside the village because even the smallest change or shift in the environment could mean something big. And very soon, they were rewarded. On one of their patrols, a team of ten jawans noticed two men nonchalantly loading a steel trunk into a Jeep. The jawans stealthily surrounded the vehicle, and the culprits were shocked when they loaded the trunk, turned around, and stared into the barrel of an AK-47. They tried to jump from the other side and walked into the waiting arms of three more soldiers. When searched, the Jeep yielded an AK-47 and a pistol, and the trunk yielded 50 lakhs in hard cash. The entire group along with the the driver, the weapons, trunk, cash, and the two terrorists were brought to the camp. Here the two terrorists confessed that they had robbed a nearby bank and had just loaded the money into the trunk and the trunk into the Jeep when they ran into the Army patrol. Or rather, the patrol ran into them. Vijay and the rest of the jawans, all from middle to lower-middle-class families, had not seen so much cash together in one place. Vijay remembered being very uncomfortable in the presence of so much cash and was happy when the bank claimed it back the next morning. A week later, a Delta Company platoon recovered a large stash of drugs. Bank robberies and the drug trade are both commonly used means to fund terrorism. With these recoveries, the Delta Company closed a major source of terror funding in their district.

But the best chapter of the company was yet to be written. And it had a close relationship with food. It is said that an Army marches on its stomach. When soldiers left their camp for operations and daily surveillance, the target areas were at least 15 km from the camp. The team usually either walked through fields or took public transport. And since these operations continued the whole day, the soldiers always carried food wherever they went. Usually, it was either solid food or Puris with aloo ki sabzi. By the time they reached their destination, the cooked food would get cold, and it did not have the same taste as the meal prepared in the morning.

Vijay noticed the resigned looks as the jawans opened their food packets and looked at the unappetising blob that they had to eat for lunch. Vijay realised that he needed to think out of the box to figure out how to get his men hot food when they were in the middle of an operation. He thought of a plan. He went to the market and bought two huge steel trunks, the kind that was used to carry clothes and other materials. Along with his JCOs, he insulated the insides to make sure that things inside stayed warm for a long time. Then he bought two locks. He gave one key to his cook, and he carried the other with him. And finally, he recruited a local who owned a truck. This guy would be responsible for delivering the food from the camp to wherever the company was conducting their operation.

Now, instead of carrying the food, they carried dry ration for the road. The cook prepared the meal an hour before lunchtime and packed them inside the insulated trunks along with flasks of steaming hot tea. He then locked the trunks and put a seal on the lock. The truck driver carried the two trunks loaded with food to the site of operation. So, every time the group of soldiers took a break from their operations, they were welcomed with hot food and a steaming cup of chai. The truck driver who bought the food was given the first bite to eat so that the chances of the food being poisoned along the way were zero.

This small experiment had a tremendous effect on the company. In a cold harsh region like Kashmir, the soldiers got hot food during their daily excursions away from the camp.

This was a game-changer beyond Vijay's imagination. Now the men felt that not only did their leader lead from the front and discipline them, but he also cared for them. Both their performance and their well-being mattered to someone. And if it did, then they had to reciprocate. While providing one additional hot meal seemed like a symbolic gesture, the intention and ingenuity that went behind it started showing results.

Vijay started getting friendly calls from other company commanders complaining to him that the troops in their companies had started asking why couldn't they have the same arrangement that Delta Company had.

As they moved from one success to another, Vijay paid close attention to the villages around the camp that they occupied. The camp was surrounded by a few villages, and Vijay had seen how the villagers lived in abject poverty. They did not have money to buy rations, and some of them survived on a single meal a day. Inside the camp, it was common for soldiers to load their plates with more food than what they intended to eat and waste the rest. Vijay convinced the soldiers to take less food on their plates and come for seconds if needed. The cook started noticing that the consumption fell, and they were consuming 20 percent less ration than before. Vijay called the JCO and told him, "Saab, use the remaining ration and prepare a meal. Then let's go and distribute this food among the villagers. A lot of them will have a second meal that day. A luxury that they can rarely afford." The JCO, who by now knew how his boss thought, did not argue. That evening the Delta Company soldiers went around and started distributing food to the impoverished villagers. The villagers initially were suspicious and refused to take the food. Vijay persisted and realised that slowly it was the hungry village children and their mothers who came forward to accept the food. Innocent children rarely carry hatred in their hearts. After that day, no child in any of the neighbouring villages ever slept hungry. Acting from the goodness of his heart, Vijay was not aware of the seeds that his actions had sown.

Three months later, two elders from a nearby village walked up to the Army camp and requested a meeting with the Company Commander. When Vijay sat them down, over a cup of tea, they nervously informed him that a large meeting was called by the local Lashkar-e-taiba commander with his senior terrorist leaders. And these two men were asked to vacate their homes to accommodate the terrorists and also organise a feast in their honour. The irony was not lost on the men and their families. The terrorists who were apparently fighting on their behalf kicked them out of their house, whereas the Army, who were the enemy, fed their children.

The next day six hardcore militants got together in the house. The neighbouring house was used as a decoy, and they posted five sentries around to warn them of any danger. The "towlia," "tel," and coughing into the sleeves training ensured that, while these five sentries were silently taken out, the six terrorist leaders were blissfully unaware that their time on this earth was coming to an end. The Delta Company troops surrounded the house, and a couple of grenades that landed in the middle of a heated discussion happening in the house prematurely ended it. Only two terrorists survived that explosion, and by the time the gun battle ended in the morning, they too were eliminated. The tight cordon by the soldiers of the Delta Company, reinforced by troops from other companies of their Battalion, ensured that no terrorist could escape. When the dust settled, Vijay was thankful that he did not lose any of his soldiers. They killed eleven terrorists, six of them hardcore terrorist commanders. In that instant, Vijay knew that these villages in his AOR would not harbour any terrorists any time soon. He and his men did not celebrate.

They sanitised the area, collected all arms and ammunition that they could find, and handed over the bodies of the dead terrorists to the local police. And when Vijay looked at his CO and soldiers from the other companies of the RR Battalion, he saw in their eyes an emotion that he had never seen before: deep admiration for the brave men of the Delta Company. A bunch of stragglers who transformed themselves into the regiment's most successful fighting force in a mere 6 months.

Author's note: Col. S Vijay Kumar SM (retd) had a very successful tenure as the Delta Company commander. Under his leadership, the company was honoured with a Shaurya Chakra, India's third-highest peacetime gallantry award, and he himself was awarded a Sena Medal gallantry for outstanding gallantry and leadership. Vijay eventually rose to command the storied 8 Mahar regiment as a full Colonel. His last posting was as a Colonel at the NDA, from where he passed out as a young Cadet years ago. After many years of service, Vijay hung up his Army boots and is currently working in the private sector..

Chapter 9
The Men Who Saw Tomorrow

*Long-term thinking is a rare skill among leaders, especially in today's world, where many leaders are trying to focus on actions that can maximise near-term impact. But we all have deep respect for those leaders who have the **vision to think long-term**, and who take decisions that can benefit people for generations to come. This is the story of such leaders in the Indian Air Force who took a bold decision in 2008 that immensely benefited the nation nearly a decade later, years after they had retired.*

Group Captain Suryakant Chafekar was waiting nervously near the conference room of his Air Force Squadron. Air Marshal PK Barbora, the Air Officer Commanding in Chief (AOC-in-C) of the Western Air Command of the Indian Air Force (IAF), was visiting Chandigarh Air Force base for the day. Air Marshal Barbora, who was their eventual boss and reported directly to the Chief of Air Staff, IAF, had recently taken command of the Western air command and was visiting all the major air bases under his command.

The Western Air Command is IAF's largest command with over 200 air bases under its remit. Its area of responsibility stretches all the way from Rajasthan to Jammu and Kashmir and Leh, covering the states of Himachal, Punjab, Haryana, New Delhi, and western

Uttar Pradesh. The command had taken part in all the major wars and battles that India had been involved in and played an effective role as the sentinel against both our aggressive neighbours - Pakistan and China.

The Chandigarh Air Force base is IAF's premier transport hub, with medium and large transport aircraft squadrons. Group Captain Chafekar was the Commanding Officer of the No. 48 Squadron of the AN-32 medium-lift transport aircraft. And he was waiting to brief Air Marshal Barbora on his squadron operations and missions. Along with Air Marshal Barbora, Chaferkar's immediate boss, Air Commodore SRK Nair, and other senior officers will be present for the briefing. Chafekar knew his squadron in and out and could run the briefing in his sleep. And he rarely got overawed by authority.

But the cause of his nervousness was a little different. Toward the end of his presentation, he added a section that proposed a top-secret mission that no one knew about. Not even Air Commodore Nair. Chafekar was breaking strict Air Force chain of command rules, taking an idea directly to the AOC-in-C.

He was also nervous because his history with Western Air Command AOC-in-C's was not very good. He clearly remembered the incident in 2002 when he was the Captain of an AN-32 aircraft that was being piloted by the then AOC-in-C of the Western Air Command. They were supposed to take-off from the Leh airport and land at the newly created Kargil Airport. Given the proximity to the LoC (border of India and Pak-occupied Kashmir (POK)), pilots are required to maintain a strict distance of 10-15 km from the Pak-occupied side. However, the pilot, either because of confusion or bravado, strayed very close to the LoC. As per the newspaper reports, the aircraft was fired upon by the Pakistani troops who alleged that the AN-32 had strayed into the Pak-occupied Kashmir (POK) airspace. This was only three years after the Kargil War, and the tensions between both armies were running high.

The missile took out one of the engines of the AN-32, and the aircraft barely managed to limp back to the Leh airbase. The post-incident court of inquiry squarely blamed the AOC-in-C, who was asked to retire, and exonerated Chafekar. However, the resultant finger-pointing and the stress of the incident were too much for Chafekar. He asked for a less demanding NCC posting to recover his confidence. The Air Force gave him a few years to recover and brought him back to command a frontline squadron.

Chafekar brought himself back to the present as Air Marshal Barbora and his entire entourage filed into the conference room. Chafekar looked at the authoritative Air Marshal in the eye and walked him through the major highlights of the squadron's operations over the past 12 months. Barbora asked him some sharp questions which he handled well. As they were winding down the presentation, Chafekar looked at Barbora and said,

"Sir, if you don't mind and can spare another 10 minutes, I have some additional slides I want to run you by. This is an operation that I have been thinking about for the past 3 months."

The temperature in the conference room suddenly fell. Chafekar avoided looking at his immediate boss, Air Commodore SRK Nair. The astute Barbora, a veteran of many battles, both with the enemy and the Air Force bureaucracy, immediately realised that Chafekar was skating on thin ice. He also understood that unless Chafekar was stupid, what he had to say must be really important. And stupid officers don't make COs of important frontline squadrons in the Air Force.

He looked Chafekar in the eye and said, "I have all the time you need, Chafekar. Let's just make sure that it's well spent."

Chafekar moved to the next slide in the presentation. It was a map of India's northernmost part, a sea of muddy brown cut only by a white streak. In the Northeast corner of the map, on the Indian side, was a tiny dot, easy to miss unless one was searching specifically for it.

"This point, Ladies and Gentlemen, is Daulat Beg Oldie or DBO air strip as it is currently known. And I think it's time we reactivated it," Chafekar said with a flourish.

Everyone in the room stared at Chafekar as if he was mad. That is everyone, except Air Marshal Barbora. Unknown to Chafekar, Barbora had looked at a similar map hanging in his office a couple of weeks ago and wondered why the DBO air strip was still inactive.

The DBO was built by the British during the Second World War in Ladakh, more specifically on the eastern front which extends from Arunachal Pradesh to Ladakh. It is the only airstrip in India situated at an impossible height of 16,700 ft at the northeastern corner of the Karakoram Range and is regarded as an engineering marvel. It does not have a proper tarmac and on most days, the airstrip is covered by a layer of dust. On other days, it gets buried in deep snow when temperatures plummet to as low as -55 C.

It was said to be a stopping point for the Mongols who invaded India. Sultan Said Khan, a direct descendant of Tuglukh Timur had launched looting invasions to Kashmir and Ladakh in 1532. The next year, while returning to Yarkent (China) he died near the Karakorum range and it came to be known as Daulet Beg Oldi, which in Turkish literally means "spot where the great and rich man died".

After the British left, DBO became non-functional and remained so till 1962 when after the India-China war, the airstrip was briefly reactivated by landing and taking off. Since then, the DBO airstrip remained unused.

In today's world, DBO is of immense strategic importance for India. It literally lays at the base of the Karakoram Pass and has POK to its west and China to its east. Keeping DBO operational would give India some oversight over the activities of both China and Pakistan in this region.

Chafekar continued, "I can understand our reluctance. In fact, it has been more than 45 years since anyone landed a plane at this place. But I think we have waited enough."

Chafekar showed more maps. The airstrip was less than 8 kms from the Line of Actual Control (LAC), the disputed border with China that lay to the east. The next slide was alarming.

"These are some satellite pictures of the Chinese side. The DBO bowl is at 16,700 ft and the surrounding mountains exceed 22,000 ft. Beyond these mountains is the Chinese territory. And just look at the infrastructure that they have built on their side. All-weather roads, tunnels, and airstrips. They have artillery weapons and even tanks. They can move into our territory in hours, and we will take days or maybe even weeks to move troops and respond."

Chafekar paused for effect, "Sir, we have had an Army post at DBO since 1960. These troops, comprised of Army infantry, Engineers, and Indo-Tibetan Border Police (ITBP) personnel, live in inhospitable conditions. Their supplies are dropped by parachute by planes from my squadron. The only thing we can land there are small helicopters. The poor soldiers must trek for more than a week to go to Leh, a journey that will take less than 30 minutes by air."

Barbora listened patiently, "All this makes sense, Chafekar. And honestly, we have known a lot of these facts. The question is, what do you want to do about it?"

Chafekar took a deep breath. This was a make-or-break moment, "I want to land and take-off an AN-32 at DBO Sir, thereby re-activating it and starting regular supply flights there. We can then deploy and redeploy troops. I want to convert this airstrip into an Advance Landing Ground for India, the world's highest."

There was silence in the room. Chafekar looked ahead, not making eye contact with anyone.

Barbora smiled and stood up, "I like people who go against the grain. You have 2 weeks. I want you and Air Commodore Nair to come to the Western Command headquarters in Delhi with an executable plan and brief my entire team. If I like the plan, I promise that I will work with you to make it happen."

Chafekar was still reeling when he finally went back home. His wife did not need to ask him how the meeting went.

She smiled, "Looks like you will have your hands full in the coming few weeks?"

Chafekar looked lovingly at his wife, who was his rock and uncomplainingly supported him through all the difficult phases of his Air Force career. Although she did not know the specifics of the operation, she could sense that her husband was planning to do something big and risky, that could destroy his career and their collective peace of mind, if it did not go well. Chafekar deeply valued the fact that his family had his back.

The next day he briefed the other officers in his squadron. He told them that the AOC-in-C is now expecting a plan from them in 2 weeks that could have long-term ramifications for the defence of our country. He and his men had already worked out the initial plan. It was time to make it fail-proof.

Chafekar, his boss SRK Nair, and a small contingent from the Chandigarh Air Force base reached the Western Air Command HQ for a briefing to Air Marshal Barbora and his staff officers. The plan was two-fold:

1. Making the unused airstrip ready for landing a heavy AN-32 transport aircraft. This involved cleaning the rocks and loose gravel. Any undulations on the land need to be levelled and holes need to be filled. The landing strip then will be tested for strength so that the aircraft won't sink into the ground after it lands. There was no need to clear any vegetation, as not even a blade of grass grew at those heights. And the actual runway will be, as before, an unpaved surface without any asphalt.

2. The other part of the plan involved the actual aircraft that Chafekar would land. The AN-32 is a twin-engine turbo-prop medium-lift aircraft of Ukrainian origin that formed the backbone of IAF's transport fleet. It is a rugged aircraft design and can easily take-off from unpaved dirt runways. It can carry about 50 fully equipped troops and can fly at a maximum height of 31,000 feet. The issue with operating at high-altitude airfields like DBO is that the air density decreases, and this meant landing at higher speeds than what Chafekar will land at airports like Chandigarh. The low air density also makes taking off harder, and the aircraft will need a longer runway to take-off. Chafekar's team carefully calibrated runway lengths, landing distance, and finally

the aircraft weight. The objective was to remove excess weight from the aircraft. The team also realised that once they land at DBO, they will have to keep the aircraft engines running. Because the oxygen levels were very low at those heights, once shut down, the engines couldn't be restarted. The recurring nightmare that Chafekar had for a few days before the operation was that he landed successfully at DBO, and was unable to take-off, thereby stranding a multimillion-dollar IAF aircraft on a desolate airfield.

The neatly cut grass under Air Marshal Barbora's shoes crunched as he made his way across the lush landscape towards the 2 men in the distance. Unlike the two men who were dressed in tees and trousers, he was in his uniform. After his meeting with Chafekar and the team, Barbora knew that he would need blessings and support from these two men to make this operation happen.

"Ah, Barbora, care for a game of golf?" said one of the men as he positioned to take the next shot. He was the Air Force Chief, and whenever the opportunity presented itself, he came to the Delhi Golf Club to play golf with some of his friends. Today it was his counterpart in the Army, The Army Chief of Staff.

The Air Marshal smiled. "No Sir. I'm on duty. Sorry to bother you on a Sunday, but this is urgent."

"Well, go on then."

"Sir, my team and I are working on a plan to reactivate DBO. Need support from both of you to make it happen."

The Air Chief paused midway, his club raised in the air. He looked at the Air Marshal and then in one swing struck the golf ball, sending it flying.

"Shot!" exclaimed the Army Chief with a wide grin. He knew where this conversation was going.

"Hmm… I see," the Air Chief said, keeping his expression neutral.

"Sir, instead of taking permission from the Ministry of Defence, I want to just go ahead and do one round of landing and take-off from the airstrip. That will officially reactivate it. We can ask for forgiveness later if we come under fire."

The Chief was taken aback. To seek forgiveness in the military was a bold thing to do. Not many had the guts to take such a drastic step. Also, Air Marshal Barbora had no reason to take such a huge risk and put his reputation on the line. He had only a couple of years left before his retirement, and anyone else in his shoes would have quietly let the days pass.

"Is the airstrip ready?" the Air Chief asked.

"No Sir." Barbora replied and turned to the Army Chief. "Sir, we will need a lot of support from the Army to get it ready. Only the Army soldiers on the ground can make it happen."

The Army Chief looked sharply at Barbora and said, "This is a bold move Barbora. The Army will give you whatever you need to make it happen."

The Air Chief added, "It's your AOR; you are free to do whatever you want to do there, Barbora. Hope you are successful. Godspeed."

The team hit the ground running. The indomitable Army engineers worked at breakneck speed to get the airstrip ready. Chafekar, on his helicopter recces, saw that the Army personnel were manually pushing and pulling small rollers to even out the ground. He was amazed because it was impossible for him to breathe without occasional oxygen support while he was on the airstrip. The oxygen levels were so low that Air Marshal Barbora's lighter wouldn't light. Yet these Army personnel were walking up and down the strip with a heavy roller.

Chafekar eventually landed in the helicopter to check the strength of the field. As he was walking on the strip, a young Ladakhi ITBP soldier walked up to him.

"Bura na maano toh ek baat poochoon Saab? If you don't mind, can I ask you something?"

"Go ahead," Chafekar said.

"Saab, I come from a small village in Leh and have been serving here for the past 3 years. Before me, my father also worked at this airstrip for over 20 years. It takes us almost 10-12 days to trek back to the village. Going home on chutti (leave) almost felt like a punishment."

Both Chafekar and the soldier smiled at the irony.

The soldier then turned serious. "But that's ok Saab. We know what we are getting into when we volunteer to serve at this place. But every once in a while, a Saab like you turns up, showing us hopes and dreams that never get fulfilled. So, my question for you is this, 'Will we finally have air connectivity to Leh or will you make a few more helicopter trips and disappear.'"

Chafekar looked into those honest fearless eyes, "What is your name, son?"

"Namgyal Saab." The soldier replied.

"This much I can promise to you Namgyal." In a few weeks from now, I will land that plane, feed you mithai with my very own hands, and then take-off. Go tell your family that from now on, while on chutti, you will reach home in under a day."

Namgyal's face broke into a wide grin, "I will be waiting for you Saab."

On the designated day, the team got up early. By 3:00 AM, the 48 squadron was a beehive of activity. To maximise engine performance by the time they reached DBO, the take-off from Chandigarh was planned for 4:50 AM. Air Marshal Barbora had reached Chandigarh the previous evening. He and Chafekar had an early dinner. As the plates were being cleared, the Air Marshal looked at Chafekar and said, "Chafi, I want to be on that plane tomorrow as we land at DBO."

Chafekar was surprised. He was proud that the man who made all this happen wanted to be at the frontlines when his team finally executed the plan. But a part of Chafekar was also nervous. He remembered that fateful day in 2002 when another Air Marshal was in command of his aircraft, and Chafekar felt he did not have the authority to make critical decisions.

Barbora read his mind, "Don't worry Chafi. This will be different. I will tag along as a passenger on the aircraft. You will be the pilot in command. All decisions are yours. Honestly, if you decide not to land because the conditions don't support it, I am happy for you to abort the mission."

"And also, I don't need special seats and other comforts. I will sit on the side benches, the way our soldiers do."

Chafekar's respect and admiration of his AOC-in-C grew manyfold. The message it will send to everyone in the squadron, at DBO, and the Air Force will be enormous.

On the 31st of May 2008, the AN-32 lifted off on schedule from Chandigarh and made its way to DBO, crossing over the high Himalayan peaks over Ladakh. Accompanying this was another An-32 flown by Air Commodore Nair, which acted as a weather recce to check the weather at the destination. It also was used to keep an eye out for any activity from the Chinese side of the LAC.

A little after 6:00 AM, Chafekar's An-32 broke through the clouds at 20,000 ft and entered the DBO bowl. As he lined up with the runway, landing at a speed that was twice as fast as he usually did, Chafekar realised that this was the moment that he and his team were training for all their lives in the Air Force. He had just one shot at landing his plane. He did not have enough fuel to attempt another landing on this mission.

Exactly at 6:14 AM, the heavy AN-32 made an expectedly bumpy landing at DBO, the first time an aircraft landed there since 1962. Chafekar turned around at the end of the runway and kept the engines running. He and Air Marshal

Barbora got down from the aircraft and were received by senior Army officers and soldiers. Barbora distributed the sweets he got for the brave Army and ITBP soldiers from Chandigarh. The atmosphere was very festive.

Chafekar beckoned young Namgyal over, who walked up with tears in his eyes and accepted the packet of sweets that Chafekar gave him. This Saab kept the promise he made.

The mission was still half done. The DBO airfield can be reactivated only after a successful landing and a take-off. The AN-32 was loaded with some senior Army officers and a few soldiers. Chafekar moved the engine power to full throttle and the aircraft began to slowly move down the runway. Its propellers churned a large cloud of dust as the aircraft struggled to accelerate. But the runway was long, and Chafekar was calm. The acceleration improved, and the AN-32 slowly hit take-off speed. As he lifted off, from the corner of his eye, Chafekar saw a lone figure at the end of the runway energetically waving him on. He smiled. Namgyal's future chuttis would no longer seem like a punishment.

Author's note: The indefatigable resolve of IAF pilots and the Army's display of die-hard spirit in preparing the runway at such altitude was a true example of "jointmanship" in the armed forces and made this historical landing possible. The two intrepid Air Force officers and their team did not stop at

DBO. They reactivated two other landing grounds at Fuk-Che and Nyoma, both near the LAC. Air Marshal Barbora retired in 2010. Grp Captn., later Air Vice Marshal Suryakant Chafekar retired in 2017, capping a phenomenal career. As predicted by AVM Chafekar, in early 2020, China intruded into the Indian side of the LAC with a large number of troops. India was able to quickly build up its troop strength to almost 61,000 troops along with vehicles and tanks in a matter of days using the Advanced landing grounds at DBO, Nyoma, and Fuk-Che. AVM Chafekar was honoured with a Shaurya Chakra for leading the operation to reactivate DBO. During multiple conversations with the authors, he remained proud, yet humble about his achievements and the support he received from the Air Force and especially from Air Marshal Barbora. Readers can learn more about his life in his Memoir: Shades of Blue. Unfortunately, before this story could be published, we lost Air Marshal Barbora who passed away on the 30th of October 2023 after a short illness. We dedicate this chapter to him and his memory.

About the Authors

Purav Gandhi

Purav Gandhi is a physician by education, entrepreneur by profession and an avid military and cricket fan at heart. He currently runs a management consulting firm called Healthark Insights, that he started in 2015. Purav was introduced to the fascinating and inspiring world of armed forces when he first visited the National Defence Academy in Pune in 2018. Since then, he has read several books on military leaders and lessons from their inspiring actions, and taken every opportunity to visit various armed forces establishments across the country interacting and learning from real life heroes. He currently lives in his home town Ahmedabad, with his family that includes his parents, wife and two lovely kids.

About the Authors

Sudeep Krishna

Sudeep Krishna has worked for over 20 years in the corporate sector. Till recently, he worked as a Senior Partner in one of the world's leading Management consulting firms. While growing up in Jammu, J&K, Sudeep was exposed to the world of the Armed forces that inspired him to apply for the National Defence Academy. Having cleared the written examination, Sudeep was unable to clear the Services Selection Board (SSB) interviews. However, his interest in the armed forces never left him. As he collected many armed forces stories over the years, and these now have taken the form of this book. He currently lives in Hyderabad with his family that includes his wife and two kids.